Writing in Place

stories from the pandemic

featuring
The Literary Posse
& Writers Block Party

Editor
Barbara DeMarco-Barrett

Cover design, logo, and typography by Travis Barrett
TravisBarrettCreative@gmail.com
TravisBarrett.MyKajabi.com

Copyright © 2020 by Barbara DeMarco-Barrett

All rights reserved. No part of this book may be reproduced in any form or by any electronic or mechanical means, including information storage and retrieval systems, without permission in writing from the publisher, except by a reviewer who may quote brief passages in review.

For information about permission to reproduce selections from this book, or any other questions, email info@marsstreetpress.com.

Printed in the United States of America
First edition

ISBN: 978-0-578-78566-0

Typeset in Garamond

For Richard Dale Barrett and all those who have perished due to COVID-19.

Contents

SKOG / *Dina Andre*	1
Love in the Time of COVID / *Nancy Carpenter & Phil Doran*	17
Distance Hugging / *Cindy Trane Christeson*	31
A-Vax / *Angela Cybulski*	39
Psychopomp / *Amelia Dellos*	47
One's Company, Two's a Crowd / *B. DeMarco-Barrett*	59
Legacy / *Anne Dunham*	72
Make a Wish / *Jennifer Irani*	89
Community Spread / *Stephanie King*	102
Mary and Joseph / *Jan Mannino*	119
Womb / *Rosalia Mattern*	122
New Talents / *Marla Noel*	136
Demon / *Lisa Richter*	151

Maximum Life Span / *Dianne Russell*	156
Letting Go / *Catherine Singer*	161
Antimatter / *Marrie Stone*	169
Rats, Bats, and a Blue-Eyed Cat / *Laurie Sullivan*	190
Safe / *Judy Wagner*	202
About the Contributors	220

Foreword

On July 16, 2020, my father-in-law Richard Dale Barrett died from COVID-19. His wife did not want me to write an obituary and she put off his military funeral until Spring. This saddened me. How do we mark a loved one's passing if not with written as well as physical memorials?

It made me wonder how will we mark this time we're living through—as if we could ever forget. When the idea floated about to create a journal with fiction and nonfiction, it felt perfect. My private workshop students in the Literary Posse and the Writers Block Party jumped at the idea, too.

Hence, *Writing in Place: Stories from the Pandemic*, took root. The theme expanded to include past pandemics or—horror of horrors—one in the future.

While this book doesn't exactly mark my father-in-law's passing, it *is* a marker of this time and what we're continuing to endure. Included are dark stories, as you would imagine, as well as light pieces, stories of hope, and a mystery.

I'm proud of this anthology, put together in record time. I'm proud of all the writers who came through with great writing and compelling stories, and I'm gratified that you, the reader, have chosen to give it your attention.

Barbara DeMarco-Barrett
October 2020
Corona del Mar, California

SKOG

Dina Andre

2024

Six-year-old Freya stands next to Ella, who is washing a dish in the kitchen sink. Freya's blond curls are a small pile on top of her head with the sides and back of her head shaven. Her sister, Ella, has the same hairstyle, but her curls are dark and wild. The pair resemble sheared lambs, petite soft creatures standing in a room of filtered light.

At 17, Ella is fine-boned, small for her age. Freya is already half as tall. "Sissy, when can we go outside?" she asks, leaning against her sister.

"Frey, don't call me Sissy. Call me by my name."

"Ok, Ella," Freya says under her breath.

"Here, you dry." Ella hands her a towel, rinses another dish, sets it in a rack.

"Tell me about HYGGE again." Freya points at embroidered letters on the towel, waves it around.

Ella is familiar with this game. "Mm... hygge means hideous and gross."

Freya giggles. "No, it doesn't!"

"It means horrible, ugly genie."

Freya belly laughs. "Say it right!"

"Ok…" Ella's voice quiets as she continues. "It means happy, a cozy moment in time. Mama used to say it's like an invisible hug. You were just a baby then, with us, Mama, Papa, Uncle Alex."

Satisfied, Freya wads up the towel without drying a thing and hands it to Ella. "When can we go in the skog," she pleads.

Two golden dogs, Olaf and Anja, laze by a backdoor. They lift their heads at the word skog, perking up for a walk in the forest.

"We can go tomorrow," Ella promises, then asks, "Freya, why can't you call me Sissy?"

"Because out there they can't know I'm your sister because I might be a Munee, like you." Freya is matter of fact, unflinching. "Because there is a virus bug that kills you if you aren't a Munee."

"And…" Ella probes.

"There are Munee Hunters who want to catch us." Freya rolls her pastel blue eyes, changes the subject. "Tomorrow!" She claps. "Will we see Uncle Alex?"

"Nope," Ella says. In thought, she sits down and rubs her palm along the floor — it is hit and miss, cracked and chipped tiles in some places with a plywood subfloor exposed in other places. Her parents had the house built on a piece of property eight miles from a nearest neighbor and ten miles from town, perched like a fairy tale home at the edge of a woodland oasis stretching out from the backyard. The kitchen and great room flowed together, at one time filled with a white dining table surrounded by scoop chairs and a loveseat with scattered throw pillows splashed with images of things Ella has never seen in actual life: a seahorse, a hibiscus, a pink flamingo. There once were decorations: vases filled with wildflowers, spices and herbs in mason jars, shelves above the counter lined with colorful dishes and bowls and cups and goblets.

Until 4 years ago, when home became bunker. Her father boarded up the house, leaving one habitable area, a true family room. A queen-sized mattress lay on the floor under a picture window with a goose down comforter tucked under the edges. A folded cot is jammed next to a stainless-steel refrigerator. A bright yellow table with two chairs takes up the middle of the room. Four matching chairs line against a wall, with the television hanging above on a swinging arm. The TV sound is mute, but a Chyron runs words along the bottom of the screen as it ticks censored news. Entertainment broadcasting is a thing of the past. Dozens of books line a tall bookcase, in company with an array of DVD's scattered on a shelf next to a player. Bedding, towels, and clothing, all crammed in the pantry along with rows of canned beans, canned fruit, bags of rice, boxes of cereal, cookies, dog food.

Today Ella has few thoughts of places filled with lovely things. She has fragmented recollection, with memories eclipsed by the past several years of dark images. She has one thing: *remember the place where family and friends gather.* A note from her mother scrawled on the back of a photograph of them all together. *Hygge,* it said. *Don't forget.*

Ella turned 13-years old in January 2020. The same month a novel virus arrived and ended Hygge. Ended the mood of coziness and comfort. Ended the gift of conviviality and contentment. A pandemic ensued, forcing her family into a world of disturbed peace and inhospitality.

Her father, Zak Darwish, was a measured man from a war-torn past. Destruction of lives was not novel to him. *A virus doesn't care, it just does what it does to survive itself, but in time, it will not be our biggest concern,* he explained as he went into overdrive preparing for trouble. In contrast, her mother, Marjorie, clung to philosophy and art as she earmarked her favorite books, cited poetry, tore pages and slipped them into a notebook tucked in a kitchen drawer.

She lays a blossom over the children
covers them with the palm of her hand
No one has died of love
There is a storm like I have never felt.
—*Johanna Ekström*

The new decade unfolded as the virus seeped into the world with a silent spread, carried in the respiration of people displaying no symptoms. Within six months, a more insidious danger crept into the weave of life when the pandemic paired itself to a politico infodemic. Political dogma and fierce compassion (as incompatible ingredients) created a toxic societal brew, boiled down to one commodity to slow the spread of the disease. Masks.

Being sick without knowledge, asymptomatic people transmitted lethal breath. Factions formed. Resistance groups known as Non-Maskers became indignant rebels when told by government and health-watch to cover their mouths and noses. They made it known their preference to live and die on their own terms, discounting any duty to contain the spread. Mask mandates failed as Non-Maskers battled civil liberties, demanding to choose their own fate, with no pause to dictating the fates of others. In contrast, Mask Wearers embraced civic duties to take care of one another as united citizens. They did their best to minimize contagion. All insignificant in the face of another enemy—human desire for dominance. The Darwish family became proof of this.

Two years of navigating life around the pandemic, they were in step together. It was the summer of 2022. Open Market Day came around once a month. Zak's younger brother, Alex, was visiting. They left him with toddler Freya as she slept on a blanket on the floor with Anja, a chubby arm slung over the big dog's neck, her face against the soft cushion of yellow fur.

Zak tucked a hunting knife in his boot, Marjorie grabbed pepper-spray intended for bears, and Ella strung a whistle around her neck that could blow out an eardrum. Giving no more thought to muggers, they enjoyed the morning, pedaling their bikes the ten or so miles along the only road stitched like a hem around the skog. They arrived to fenced grounds surrounding rows of canopy tents and tables for vendors selling goods. Except for the requirement to wear masks, to respect assigned guards, and to put up with drones flying overhead, market day was one of few activities that resembled pre-pandemic life.

When huge billowy clouds rolled in, Ella noticed. "Papa," she said, "summer storm?" They headed to the bikes, filled their baskets with their shopping spree: bread, cheese, smoked fish, pickles, a bottle of wine, a bunch of moon-daisies tied with a string, a tiny rabbit-puppet made from an infant sock for Freya. As they rolled to the exit, pointing at the sky to outwit one another by naming faces and animals in cloud formations, Zak stopped. He cocked his head to listen as he led them back to a corner behind a birch tree, where they huddled, leaning their bikes against the trunk. A group gathered by the exit; they were agitated with mocking tones. In timed precision they pulled off their masks and began swarming the market, spewing and spitting. Fanning out, they targeted shoppers, vendors, spat on their shoes, on their clothes, in their hair, in their faces. They outnumbered the guards. Tables tipped, tents collapsed, fighting broke out and screaming filled the market. The number of drones increased, circling above like an electric flock, buzzing and snapping.

As chaos ensued, Zak got down, grabbed Ella by the shoulders. "Run home! Don't take the road, go through the skog, zig-zag like I taught you." He turned his daughter around and gave her a little push.

Ella stayed planted for a moment, she was unafraid but there was an anguish washing over her; she didn't want to leave her parents, she didn't want to leave her bike, she didn't want to run alone, away from what was supposed to be a day of…Like Before. She wanted it all to go away, all the badness.

Zak gave her another nudge. "Go sweetheart, now…"

Ella turned, plucked the finger-puppet from her bike basket and darted for the exit. As she fled, she bore witness to a white van just outside the market grounds, with the back doors flung open. An unmasked man spit on her as she flew by. Ella disappeared into the forest, running, running with the image etching deep into her mind of children crying, being dragged by their hair towards the van.

Skog

As Zak and Marjorie began to roll their bikes, headed for the exit, a hawkish woman spotted them. She was enormous, but quick. Zak reached for the knife in his boot as she loomed over his petite wife. Marjorie fumbled in her pocket for the pepper spray and when she looked up, the woman spat in her eye. Marjorie cringed and blinked. Zak shoved the woman to the ground as she hissed like a feral cat and the bikes clattered down. A jar of pickles and a bottle of wine smashed, mingling into a blood-red spill as the attacker struggled to her feet. Zak, in a seamless motion, dove to the ground, rolled behind her, and with a heavy swipe, lacerated the back of her knee with his blade. She buckled, clutching her slashed artery, shrieking.

Zak was born boots on the ground and he had memories to ignite familiar rings of dystopian rumblings. For the past eighteen months, he had been using all he knew to strengthen his small family. He had started with boarding up the house into one space, knit together, strength in unity. As civil unrest swelled during the pandemic, he was forced into practiced response—to aggression, to looters, to two attempted home robberies, to muggers at an ATM in town, to hoarders of food and supplies threatening reason. Zak attempted to take fear out of discussions by calling these incidents, *monsters of mere nuisance*. Over and over he would say, *listen here, we are quiet courage, we are balanced conviction, we are prepared for the monsters of mere nuisance.*

But on the last beautiful market day they would share, with the sky filled with nebulous clouds, he was not prepared. Not for these monsters of mad menace, not for pure evil.

After the attack, Zak struggled with his bearings. He saw Marjorie, stunned and solo, rubbing her eyes with the edge of her sweater. He pulled the bikes up, grabbed her hand, and jostled through the exit. Riding home, full of nauseating adrenaline, his wife pedaling at his side, Zak could not stop his one thought. *A virus needs a keyhole to enter the body*, stated the World Health Organization. Don't touch your face. Everyone knew that one.

Zak coughed and sweat for days, gasping as the virus load exploded, bombarding his lungs as if he had inhaled shards of glass. Battling the illness was second to his willful battle to confer with his brother. Alex came from a lifetime of rebellion. He was familiar with how factions formed and then fragmented.

"It's complicated," Alex told Zak as they spoke in quiet. "I knew about the groups in the cities, but they've branched out. Non-Maskers are kidnapping to line their pockets, getting paid with diverted science funding. Researchers are working out why some people are immune to the virus and they want subjects. They want children. They call them Munees."

"But, you?" Zak asks.

"I know, I was exposed to the virus all over the place in the field last year." Alex's voice cracked as he viewed his older brother, dying in front of his eyes. "Some adults are immune too." He let out a heavy sigh before finishing. "Some are carriers without symptoms and the Munee Hunters use them to cause chaos. They're called Spitters."

Zak made a sound like a wounded animal, "Ella!" he said, going into a fit of coughing and pain. Alex grabbed his hand and held on. "Yes, Ella didn't get sick after the attack but only we know that. Munee Hunters take any kid, hand them over to institutes for genetic testing.

The corporations are nefarious, competing. If they get a Munee, the payoff is big." Alex paused. "Siblings are the golden ticket."

Zak struggled to respond. "Alex, go into the forest. Count thirty-three steps from the porch. Walk forward and then to the left. Take Olaf and Anja, command, *Boksen*."

"What is Boksen?"

"Box. A metal one, bring it here." Zak rolled his head to the side, observed the emptiness next to him where Marjorie once was.

Across the room, Freya sat oblivious to talk of danger as she watched her favorite movie, *Frozen*. She sang along to songs, muffled by the pink bandana tied around her nose and mouth. Ella pretended to be watching as she strained to decipher their language as Papa and Alex spoke. She twirled a bright, orange silk scarf in her hands. Tying it in knots. Untying it. Munee. She is a Munee?

"Ella, come sit with your Papa." Alex rose, whistled for the dogs. He grabbed his camo-jacket, patted the gun in his pocket, took off out the back door.

Zak closed his eyes, reached a hand up as Ella sat next to him. They rested their grasp on the damp sheets until she slipped her hand away, tucked the scarf in his palm.

"Here, Papa, this is Mama's."

Zak squeezed it as tears rolled down his cheeks. Marjorie had succumbed to an uncommon reaction to the virus with a stroke, a clot bleeding into her brain, a silent battle, a sleeping beauty. Zak followed his wife after ten more days of coaching his brother. And then he suffocated on his own breath.

Alex took care of detail. Without sharing his brother's sensibilities, he did not protect his nieces from grit. Strangers showed up, took away their parent's bodies wrapped in sheets, rolled into a truck bed, covered them in logs. Freya stood wide eyed, clinging to her finger puppet. Ella spotted the orange silk scarf flitting in the wind and blowing away. Alex used the contents of the metal box to shelter them in place. He drilled Ella, imparting information: bank accounts, cash instructions, a list of contacts (who-is-who-for-what), birth certificates, passports, protocols. He set them up for porch delivery of provisions from town. He tended the vegetable garden in the side yard and taught both girls the same. He quizzed them on memorized contact numbers and arranged for a man named Mr. C. as the go-to in case of trouble.

When the time came, Alex paid it forward. He knew what he knew—recruit training. He found a clearing deep in the skog and played it like a game. Archery, knifery, gunnery. Exercising, running, jumping, tree climbing, tumbling, fast, slow, high, low. *I started when I was 5-years old*, he would say. *And look at me now, at 25, call me Superman!* Hobbling like an old man to trip into a pile of leaves, he would make the girls laugh.

He nicknamed Freya, *Ankle-Biter*. How to escape the *monsters*, how to injure them from down low. And just in case, how to use a penknife to slash a monster behind the ear. Ella—a natural, he called Ninja. She was small but quick and resolute in every action. It made him proud, but also terrified him in the burgeoning anti-utopia. It's important to play it down, he would insist. *No one should know what you know until you need it!*

"Ella," Alex said, as they sat in the clearing on an afternoon of training, chomping on carrots and peppers from the garden. "I have to go away for a bit."

Ella didn't move. Or blink. Or speak. She swallowed a pain so deep in her throat she thought she might choke. She nodded and peered at Freya, who was running circles with the dogs. "Got it," she said.

"The hunters, they got Mr. C's son. He's watching his family, so I'm going."

"Wow." Ella sat up, stiff and straight. "That won't end well."

"Don't!" Alex raised his voice, and Ella's shoulders jumped. "Please don't." He softened. "After everything. We have to fight...for the good."

Ella looked at her uncle and saw such exhaustion, she reached to pat his shoulder. He had lost his only brother. He had stayed for the past year, all the while dealing in his secret world of fighting for the good.

"Ok, I know. I am quiet courage, I am balanced conviction, I am prepared for the monsters of mere nuisance. And ya, it's not mere nuisance anymore, it's merciless maniacs," Ella mustered up and smiled at him. "And the fighting, it's not for sport."

Alex lifted his head and smiled back at a girl who looked remarkably like him when he was a boy.

Keeping her promise, Ella dresses both herself and Freya in matching dark green jumpsuits. She pushes Freya's arms through the sleeves of a hoody sweatshirt and helps her wiggle her feet into scuffed Doc Marten's boots, the same boots Ella wore when she was 6-years old.

"Ready to race?" she says to Freya, pulling two full face respirator masks from hooks by the door. Two masks remain hanging.

Freya nods and holds her mask over her head.

"On your mark, get set, go!" They both pull the mask down over their faces, adjust the mesh headband to secure the seal to their shaven heads, then they slap their hands to their sides. They look at one another, two hornets facing off.

"You win!" Ella says, giving Freya a thumbs up. She puts on a jacket, stuffs a utility knife and some cash in her pocket and slides a key in her own Doc Marten boot. Freya skips to the door, a strand of hair stuck across her cheek. Ella lifts Freya's mask to release the curl, watches it bounce up. She fights a sense of needing to keep them locked inside. She battles her own thoughts, views them flawed somehow. It's been five months since Alex left. She tells herself that she wears a mask to avoid being seen. She puts Freya in a mask to protect for all the ways things could go wrong. How long can she keep this up? Is it senseless? Ella opens the door glancing at the framed card next to it. *Love is the whole thing. We are only pieces. –RUMI*

It just makes her head pound. Papa. Mama. Alex. Ringing in her ears.

"Olaf, Anja, let's go," she says, and the two dogs bound out headed for the trees. Ella stretches her eyes, scanning in every direction. Second nature, she has trained not to trust.

"Are we seeing Uncle Alex yet?" Freya asks as she tromps alongside.

Ella takes her sister's hand, ignoring that same constant question. "Frey, what kind of tree is that?" she asks.

"Birch!" cries Freya.

"How do you know?"

"The bark is white. And I see faces," Freya points at the peeling bark. "See, here's one."

Ella squints her eyes. So many walks, she has seen so many faces in the barks of these trees, she cannot count the mob. Now these faces are her friends, etched into the white scarred bark adorned with long swaying branches and weeping leaves.

"Yes, I see it," agrees Ella. A face between a split trunk, shaped like a heart.

"Now, how do you spell it?"

Freya yells each letter like an announcement. "B. I. R. C. H."

"Count now," Ella instructs.

Freya runs ahead. "One, two, three, four..." she counts as she runs in and out of towering trees, the aspens, the pines. Olaf and Anja run with her, barking with excitement. Ella could not see her sister's face inside the mask, but she knew it held a smile. Freya loved these games they called school.

"Stop." Ella waited. "Now, what is two plus five?"

Freya stills. The dogs sit, panting. She looks at her boots, counts on her fingers before shouting. "Seven!".

"Yep, you will be 7 years old next month."

They played all the way to the clearing, until the dogs raced ahead, growling as they circled something. Ella could see two shapes on the ground about fifteen yards away. No movement at all.

"Freya," Ella shushed. "Come here." She took Freya's hand as they ran into a thick of trees. Giving the dogs a faint whistle, she led them all to an edge of the clearing.

"Sit," she said. "Freya, if I say *GO*, then run home with the dogs. Remember the rules."

Ella skirted closer to view the figures. One was a young woman. She was lying on her side, wearing a long green trench coat and a beanie. A satchel or backpack of some sort was near her feet. Her eyes were closed, her fingers resting next to a bundle, still as stone. Ella had seen so few people in the past four years. They lived life next to and within the skog. The skog as friend and protector. The skog as training for survival. The skog as playtime, as schooltime. The skog as communion humming with hidden life. She knew it best to turn around and leave, flee, get back home away from threat. But she couldn't help herself, her mind swirled with questions and thoughts. *Is she a hunter? She looks about my age. Are there others? She is pretty. What is she doing here?* Ella felt a flutter in the pit of her stomach. Something she had not felt in years. A curious longing, wonderment.

Ella turned, looked at Freya and held her finger up. "Shhh!" She took her knife out of her boot before letting out a string of bird whistles to wake the stranger. Instead, a wailing started. The little bundle started moving until a small fist poked out of the blanket into the air.

"A baby?" Ella whispered, racing forward with Freya on her heels.

Both girls stood and studied the dead girl's face. She was alabaster pale with dark veins spidering her neck.

"What's wrong with her?" Freya asked, her voice jolting Ella to action.

She lifted the baby, cooing and calming. She showed Freya how to sit cross-legged and cradle the baby on her knees. "I did this when you were a baby," she said. "Hold your knees, now rock a little. Yes! Like that."

The dogs paced as Ella dragged the body into the brush. She then emptied the coat pockets, finding pepper spray, a baby pacifier, a small canteen of water, an even smaller bottle of milk, some cash, a number scrawled on a piece of paper. Ella stared, her heart racing. It was Mr. C's phone number. She tore it up and sprinkled the pieces in different directions and then set about scavenging for fallen pine branches and piles of leaves, enough to cover the body. Getting up from the ground, Ella paused. She walked a few feet and pulled a bunch of white wildflowers. She gazed at the covered body and sprinkled the flowers as she spoke aloud.

"*Frid vare med dig.*" Her mama would expect her to make this wish. *Peace be with you.*

They called him baby (just baby) for over three months until Ella was sure, decidedly not telling Mr. C., decidedly choosing to protect the baby as their own. The backpack in the clearing contained baby items: cloth diapers, stretchy pants, t-shirts labeled 3-6 months, a red hoodie, a wooden rattle shaped like a giraffe, a fabric Bjorn to carry him. Ella worked out the rest by adopting Alex's lead. He had pretended to be Zak as necessary, so she now pretended to be Marjorie as necessary. She added baby related supplies to their regular porch deliveries.

"Let's name him after Papa," Ella said one morning as they worked in the garden, the baby propped in a wheelbarrow, smiling and squealing at the dog's tail wagging in his face.

She walked up and leaned in. "What do you think, little Zak?"

It was then that Freya flew out of norm, became upset, broke a silence, "What about Alex? And Mama?" She pointed at the skog, and then at the sky.

Ella's stoicism cracked as her sister's lip trembled with grief. She pulled Freya close, locked eyes, struggled with what to say, what to do. "Okay. How about Z-A-M? For all of them?" she offered.

Freya nodded her head. A dimpled smile washed away the pain on her face.

"Hello there, Zam," Freya said, as she reached in and gave the baby a tiny handshake. "Some people are worth melting for," she said, borrowing a line from *Frozen,* the movie she had seen a hundred times.

Ella's lips trembled at the sweet display of affection. She took it all in, all within her reach, the fresh forest smells, the vibrant colors in the garden, the dogs at her feet, the smiles of these two small children. A feeling emerged, an awareness in the moment so remarkable, it was then she remembered: *Hygge.* A sense of well-being took over, the scars of pain subdued, and for a split-second Ella felt simplicity. She looked up as an orange scarf somersaulted in the wind out of the skog and watched it float onto the porch to land.

Love in the Time of COVID

Phil Doran and Nancy Carpenter

This is a mostly true story as recalled by the man and the woman who fell in love as COVID scrambled our world.

According to Nancy:
On June 11, 2020 Nancy receives an email.

> *Hi Nancy,*
> *I wonder if I could have your phone number? In addition to just getting to know you better, I'd like to get your opinion on what I've been writing. I think you're the smartest guy in the room and I need some help.*
> *Phil*

She's a writer. As is he. Words matter.
I wonder if I could have your phone number?
This number is in her signature block. Perhaps residing there imparts a strictly business aura, an etiquette line he's not willing to breach.
In addition to just getting to know you better....
Know her better? Surely not in the biblical sense. She's possibly as old as Sarah in the Bible.

...I'd like to get your opinion on what I've been writing.
Whatever his motivation, he's making a bid with flattery.
I think you're the smartest guy in the room and I need some help.
She's neither impressed with the reference to intelligence nor offended by the allusion to gender. "Smartest guy" is little more than slang. Phil's being flirty-flirty.

As for the room, he means the studio where their writing group meets—ten at last count, the number stable in spite of periodic flux as people join, resign, go off on self-imposed sabbaticals, disappear under the weight of frustration and rejection.

A little back story on what goes on in their writing group and *that* room, a studio with only enough space for a sofa and six chairs, three of which are comfortable. A coffee table is always laden with platters of food. Writers, like soldiers, travel on their stomach.

They share what they write. Writing is maddening and personal and private. Nothing leaves the room.

Relationships to some extent spill into their personal lives. Phil is not one of the more steadfast members, but professionally the most successful. Nancy met his wife Laura maybe a year before she became ill and within months, died. That was 2013. He's met her husband Ray at holiday events, although he doesn't recall this. Women are clearly more tuned to social integration.

They met in that room every other Thursday. They exchange tidbits of news. Everyone knew Ray's health was declining. He died the day after New Year, 2020.

Two months later, COVID began its disordering, lethal business. March 19 the writing group went from room to Zoom, their faces held captive in rows of tiny Brady Bunch frames.

Three months later, Phil's email. More on what prompted that shortly.

With or without COVID, Nancy was too raw to think about men. Besides, a pandemic's agenda is hardwired to play out in an unquantifiable length of time. Her business of grieving took a back seat. What is one deceased husband pitted against billions of other sorry stories? She knew this. She calendared the possibility of meeting someone maybe by 2022. She has one less thing to worry over for the next eighteen months.

Otherwise, she reasoned she would be okay. Her husband's passing reduced the household headcount to one, sequestering her in every way. Plus, writers have a certain advantage when it comes to quarantining. Writers are solitary performers. They isolate whenever they sit down to write. This doesn't negate a need for human interaction. And if forced into it, well, they react the same as most. They pine for what is forbidden.

She reminds herself, when critiquing someone's writing—even a humble email—stick with the words on the page.

What is it about his words that made her respond that night? Adhering to the rules of story arc, there should be a conflict. That will come.

For now, she replies and supplies.

He calls.

Phil's story:
He was once a top comedy writer in Hollywood. There, writers are akin to herds of wildebeest rotating through Eastern Africa. They were coddled and cloistered and never worked alone. Being the funniest or the smartest or the oldest guy in the room was a figure of speech that pitted talent against waning careers while maintaining a Darwinian pack-animal survivor mentality.

March 2020, Phil was bored and depressed, locked in a lifestyle without a woman to share it. A seven-year marathon with a mostly empty king-size bed. Thinking about how much fun he'd had with Laura didn't help. She loved his jokes and comedic nature, and he loved seeing her laugh. At question: Is it possible to have that simple slice of love's pie again when a man is retired and single and in his seventies?

COVID surely wasn't on his side.

He shared his frustrations with Barbara, the writing group's astute leader. She has a way with the tender hearts of writers. And a knack for this matchmaking sort of thing. To be specific, she said to him: "What about Nancy?"

Emailing Nancy was his Hail Mary. In addition to Barbara's shrewd directive, he reasoned that he lost his wife, she lost her husband. He writes, she writes. And he's anticipating she's as horny as him.

Let's leap to Phil and Nancy's first outing in public.

Two months later, Saturday evening, Laguna Beach. Marrie, a constant member of their writing group, and her husband Jeff invite them over for dinner. Faces covered, Phil and Nancy walk in and social distance in patio chairs before removing their masks so they can eat and drink. And talk. Hard to hear conversation muffled behind those things. Is that because of their age?

Dianne, also a member of their writing group, and her husband Ron are a few paces behind.

Phil and Nancy have not seen Marrie and Dianne, or hardly anyone else from the group, since the pandemic hit.

The six of them nosh on cheese balls and laugh. They mull over the status of their new world. They refrain from making a bitch fest of it.

As Marrie passes a plate of rumaki, she asks, "So what are you two crazy guys up to?"

Finally, the elephant in the room.

Phil says, "Nancy and I are now a *thing*."

Nancy says, "We're just screwing around a bit."

Marrie says, "I knew it!"

Dianne shoots a look at Marrie. "How did you know, and I didn't?" She redirects. "Let's get to it. We want the details."

"It wasn't simple," Phil says. "COVID's changed everything. I suggested a movie and dinner. She reminded me everything's closed. Phoning was our only option, but I wound up asking her inelegant questions. 'How are you feeling? Have you lost your sense of taste or smell? Can I see your last five years of blood panels?'"

Dianne says, "Good, Phil. The only thing left is birth control."

At this point, Nancy jumps in. "I felt like I was being grilled. He had all these questions on where I go, what I do. My brand of hand sanitizer. Not that they weren't legitimate questions. Who'd have thought we'd be charting temperatures? Wasn't Twenty Questions something we did fifty years ago?"

Indeed. The two of them were teenagers at a time when an unwanted pregnancy often led to an even more unwanted marriage. Birth control was a legitimate line of questioning. Then the eighties and people feared AIDS. Unlike other STDs, that was a death knell. Still, you could make choices about intimacy.

COVID is about the very air we breathe. No one has a lot of choices when it comes to breathing. Meeting for coffee is no longer a perfunctory step when pursuing someone, when ruling out those who post outdated pictures on social networking sites, their hips nesting on the fender of sports car or sipping drinks with those little paper umbrellas.

"Don't think Nancy didn't jump in with her own questions," Phil says.

"We talked on the phone every day for weeks. And I hate the phone."

"We had to be sure. This is COVID's world."

"I told him how I navigate through the grocery store," she says. "How I avoid people or at least turn away. I don't allow anyone to touch me. If they can touch me, they're too close. I'm obsessive about washing my hands and gargling with saltwater when I come home."

"The saltwater thing," Ron says. "I can remember doing that as a kid to prevent strep or something."

Nancy says, "In an odd way, all our talking made me feel safe."

"But you guys are here now," Ron says.

"Yeah," Phil says, "It wasn't without a few missteps. I finally asked her over to my place for dinner."

"You know how his retirement community is," Nancy says, "with all these curving roads and everything painted in boring beige. This is a place for older people. How can they remember where they live when everything is both confusing and the same?"

"Careful," Phil says. "Getting lost and wandering the streets is the only exercise we get."

"I found his general location, but not his home. So, I called him. He came out, and this was odd, but it occurred to me that in spite of knowing each other, I'd never seen him from a distance. And out of the context of our group." Nancy pauses for a sip of wine and to reorder her narrative. "Well, he *does* have a nice walk. The way tall people walk. Their suspension's different from shorter people. I didn't realize how tall he is."

"That is so nice and mushy," Dianne says.

"I was sort of mesmerized."

Phil says, "I got to her and touched her shoulder. Like you do normally. And she jumped."

"What'd you touch her with?" Marrie says. "Your dick?"

"Because of the pandemic, she doesn't let anyone touch her," Phil says.

"I can really feel this relationship heating up," Jeff says. "So much for the first date."

In spite of her no-touch rule, which Phil assiduously adhered to that evening, when he walked her to the car, he knew he'd call her again.

"What he didn't know," Nancy says to the group, "is I thought he must think I'm a real idiot. What kind of future is there with someone who practically decked him for touching her with his hand or whatever?"

Phil explains his approach for the second date. Saturday was the Fourth of July and a perfect excuse for barbequing filets. "I told her there probably won't be fireworks this year, which there weren't…."

"I immediately said yes. And then said something like, was that too quick? Too needy?"

"And I said, 'I'd have worried if you hesitated.' Our second date was four days later."

"Three days. It was three days."

"Ladies and gentlemen…our first argument."

"Nancy, I hope you were past the don't-touch-me rule," Jeff says.

"Actually, he ramped it up a bit," Nancy says. "I'm in the kitchen fiddling with dim sum and he's telling me some story about Laura and how he met her at a party. According to him, she was so hot she wrapped her legs around his and climbed up his body."

"This is how you met your first wife?" someone in the group asks.

Nancy ignores the comment. "He decided to demonstrate this with me."

"We're adults. Our masks were long gone. I wanted to touch her. I did an adult thing."

"And I was okay with it. But believe this, we got even more intimate."

"Are we ready for this much detail immediately before I serve the halibut?" Marrie says, uncorking a third bottle. "I need some more wine for this."

Nancy says, "We wound up on the sofa. He has this sectional, and we were both lying down, head to head but not touching. We're talking. Normal talk. No COVID talk. We're acting like two normal people in spite of everything."

Jeff says, "That's it?"

She continues. "Yeah, that was it. The intimacy of talking. In person, without masks. We were long past the interrogation phase. It was wonderful."

"It was getting late," Phil says. "Nancy has this big dog. This poodle that needed her attention. It was time to walk her to her car. There was this huge, not-to-be-ignored moon hanging in the sky."

"It was gorgeous."

"The moon was aligned with Jupiter and Saturn. I was caught up in the moment. Like I was standing on some stage set, I waxed poetic about the planets trailing the moon on a celestial highway."

Dianne says, "You actually said that to her? Geez."

"Look, I'm a writer. I don't believe in omens or miracles, but I was so moved by the synchronicity of the evening. When we got to her car, I kissed her. I had no choice."

"I was shocked," Nancy says laughing. "He's wrapped around me again. And now he's kissing me. It's a pandemic. Aren't there rules about kissing? This retirement community is pretty specific about masks. I was sure somebody was watching us."

Phil puts a stop to Nancy's monologue. "But the kiss was great."

"I get in the car and drive away."

"The kiss was great, right?"

"This community has so many exits. Wouldn't you know, the one I knew best was locked. It's after eleven. I'm thinking I'm stuck for the night sleeping in my car. And yes, the kiss was great, and I was sort of liking what was going on, but really, to go back to Phil's house?"

"Nancy finally figured out the gate matrix and got home," Phil says. "I know this because I called her to be sure. We had a long talk and she invited me to her place for the next night."

Date Three is not shared with the group. Let's cut to the day, a Sunday, between Dates Two and Three, and how things are going for Phil.

It is midafternoon and he is channel surfing, looking for a baseball game when he stumbles into a sitcom he once worked on. His old world. The first joke hits its punchline, the audience laughs but he doesn't. A second follows and he smiles, shaking his head in appreciation. The third joke comes and he's laughing mindlessly. He picks up the phone and calls Nancy.

"Hi, Phil."

"Guess what? I'm laughing."

"Okay." She stretches a simple word into three syllables.

This is Phil's pivotal moment in their budding relationship.

"I'm laughing and I'm actually happy. No, let me correct that. I'm joyously happy. And I need to tell *you*. Because the only thing that's different in my life *is you*."

That's not the only epiphany in Phil's day. He's in love. He's in like. He's in lust. He's run out of L-words. He theorizes that at his age, he shouldn't waste time.

Nancy is having her own epiphanies. The COVID business has created what she sees as a new medical condition following a recent loss of a husband: Griefus Interruptus, its most prominent manifestation random outbursts of unprovoked emotion. Plus, her life has been shrinking. A pandemic can do that.

At 4:53 that Sunday afternoon she realizes she has not had one spontaneous meltdown. For this singular day she's had no reason to cry. In fact, she too has something to smile about. Last night she was the recipient of an unselfish kiss. She touches her finger to her lower lip where surely some remnant of Phil's DNA lingers. There's no mistaking the message behind that kiss.

That evening he arrives at her home with a bottle of white wine and a bouquet of sunflowers. She is charmed. Sunflowers are a happy flower.

They work their way through a ravioli dish. He's an appreciative eater and requests seconds but will never adequately recall the mix of sweet peppers and onion with blush marinara sauce. In spite of his instincts for language and dialogue, his mind is on other matters. The specifics of their conversation will likewise blur into a fuzzy but not unpleasant memory.

As he helps clear the table, he seamlessly resurrects his monologue on planetary synchronicity.

"You're really hung up on the moon," Nancy says, balancing dishes in the sink.

"Ever since I was a kid. I'd stare up at that big, white ball and feel anything is possible." he says. He's also busy figuring out if her eyes are green with a gold tint or the other way around.

What is clear, he senses she is a bit anxious, possibly because of his earlier confession about the difference she has already made in his life. "Look, if I came on a little strong, I don't want us to lose a chance at happiness."

She says, "This business of being single is pretty fresh. The rules are different now. And even if they weren't, I know what I want to do. I'm not sure how to get there."

"That makes two of us," he says before clearing his throat. "Sometimes when writing, you say to yourself, first take care of getting the what down. Then work on the how."

"When do we take care of the when?"

"The when is now," he says.

Nancy let's this sink in. But Phil is moving forward in his usual inimitable way. She sees that look of determination she has grown fond of.

He breaks the silence. "This has been such a great night. Better than last night. Even the moon is brighter."

"You want to look at the moon again?"

"I'd rather look at you."

Nancy smiles. "Well, you can do both. We can see the moon from my bedroom."

It's a short walk down the hall with the dog trailing behind.

"Is he joining us?"

"He's been with me for years, but there are certain things he shouldn't see."

She gives the dog a look. He reluctantly retraces his steps.

When they get to her bedroom, Phil notices a blanket covering most of the bed. "It's summer. A blanket seems like a bad idea," he says, lifting one corner. "Wow, this is really hefty."

"I just got it," Nancy says. "One of those heavy-weighted blankets. It gives a sense of security that's supposed to help you fall asleep."

"I haven't been sleeping so well either. Can I…?" Phil says.

"Sure. Take off your shoes and try it."

He lies on his back and she covers him. He turns to her. "This is really heavy. But it's actually quite nice. Why don't you join me?"

She slips in next to him.

At first the blanket delivers what was promised. The weight is reassuring as it pins arms and legs to the bed.

Arms and legs are important players when it comes to bedroom activity.

"I think I enjoyed your ravioli a little too much. I need to unbuckle my pants, but I can't move my hands."

"Let me help." She fumbles a bit with the buckle. "You're right. Damnit."

He reaches down to try again, not willing to give up on the moment. "I almost got it."

He turns to her and clearly sees—her eyes are green with a gold tint. It's a kiss-worthy moment not impacted by the blanket. When he's satisfied that he has efficiently explore what he has deemed a very lovely mouth, she smiles and says, "Let me try that buckle with my teeth."

Thus unencumbered, they make love. Phil finds a place on her neck he has yet to kiss.

"That was...," she starts to say before Phil interrupts with his own "I know."

She mumbles a bit more.

"I believe you're trying to say, you've just had some good fucking. And...you enjoyed it."

Nancy feels she got that and more.

And so, Phil who has been dating a number of women without ever using the word love, now tells Nancy how much he does love her, every day.

Nancy watches Phil in fascination as he shaves in the shower. He often finds room for her.

Thus, two crazy kids camouflaged as old people, collecting social security and waiting for the first COVID vaccine courtesy of Medicare, find themselves in love. In like. In lust. Like everyone, they have been looking for a bit of hope for the future. They have not lost sight of the billions of sad stories. There is guilt, too, for having this happiness in the time of COVID.

We need optimism for the future, and the belief in a better after-pandemic world. Theirs arrived a bit sooner.

Distance Hugging:
Comforting Grievers During a Pandemic
Cindy Trane Christeson

"Sometimes I miss my mommy so much, my body aches, and I just have to cry," my four-year-old granddaughter Mary said to me one morning after bursting into our room. Mary's parents were out of town, due to return that night. I opened the covers and invited her in. Her eyes were damp.

"What do you do when I'm sad," I said, "and missing Aunt Amy?"

"I hug you," she said, while snuggling into my waiting arms.

While her mother, my daughter, Kelly, would be back soon, my other daughter, Amy, would never return. She died in a car accident a year before, and Mary had an innate sense of knowing when I needed a hug, often seconds before I began to cry. I felt deep comfort each time her chubby little arms reached around me.

My friends and family hugged me a great deal, too, and each hug went deep to my soul. Hugs were an important part of my healing. This happened thirteen years ago, long before I'd heard of social distancing and distance learning.

What do we do when we can't hug each other during a pandemic? How do we comfort grievers without the comfort of physical touch?

During the pandemic, we've experienced life in ways we never imagined. But far too many also experience death, and grieve in ways never imagined, either.

We learned new ways to market, to work, and to live; we can learn new ways to mourn, to grieve, and to adjust to death when it comes.

We can learn to hug without touching. We can distance hug during a pandemic.

Hug with your presence After Amy died, friends showed up, and their presence was a gift. During a pandemic, you can still show up, just in different ways. The mother of a friend named Jane contracted COVID-19 while in a senior facility, but Jane wasn't able to visit her because of the lockdown. We couldn't visit Jane either, but a group of us texted or emailed our ongoing concern and prayers. We frequently asked how she was doing and arranged meetings by Zoom so we could connect. We had a Zoom call after Jane's mom passed and let her share her feelings. Later we hugged Jane with our presence by watching the live-streaming memorial for her mother.

The pandemic may have robbed grievers of the usual rituals, but there are still ways to honor and remember loved ones who die. On-line memorials can have all the ingredients of the normal services, just on a smaller scale. People can "attend" from across the country, or around the world.

Other ways to make your presence known to grievers is by leaving notes, flowers, or thoughtful gifts on their doorstep. One friend left a grieving friend a 12-pack of toilet paper tied with a bow, a unique and appreciated gift near the beginning of the pandemic. Pandemic or not, grievers always appreciate condolence cards.

Hug with your ears   Show your concern for the griever by showing interest in the one they mourn. "Tell me about Amy," friends said to me after Amy died. It meant so much that they weren't afraid to say Amy's name, and I was thankful that they wanted to know about her. We asked Jane to tell us about her mother, to share stories. We walked down memory lane with her. The more she spoke about her mom, the more animated her voice became. We came to know Jane's mother better through Jane's recollections. We also learned more about their relationship.

"She made me crazy sometimes, you know, but she was my mom," Jane said, and chuckled. We joined in the laughter. I almost forgot we weren't in the same room together.

Grief can make grievers feel alone, and the weight of sadness often pushes grievers to further isolate. We all struggle with isolation during a pandemic, so pandemic grievers need others to find creative ways to build a sense of community and connection. Grievers need to mourn with others.

Hug with your eyes   "Can you show us a picture of your mom, Jane?" I asked at one of our Zoom check-ins. A smile formed on Jane's face, and she popped up from her chair with new energy. "I'll be right back," she said as she disappeared from our screens. She was back shortly with several photos of her mother at different ages. She proudly held up one photo after another in front of her computer, eagerly sharing additional stories and memories.

Hug with acceptance   A friend named Tracey also lost her mother during the pandemic. Sometime later, I saw Tracey in person at a socially distanced event. As I told her how sorry I was, tears formed in her eyes. Tracey looked embarrassed and started saying she was sorry.

"Please don't apologize," I said. "Your mom is worth crying over. You are honoring your mother with your tears."

Tracey appreciated permission and encouragement to cry. Grievers need to talk, and often need nudges from others to do so. They also need to cry. I'm not sure why we think we shouldn't cry. Losing a loved one is a pain unlike anything else. The ache is piercing. Devastating. Grievers need to vent sadness through their tears. Some try to stuff their churning sorrow for a time, but grief will force its way out at some point, in some way. Ungrieved grief doesn't go away. It can manifest itself later in depression or illness.

Hug without judgment   Jane's mother died without Jane ever getting to visit her, hold her hand, or stroke her hair. Jane wrestled with anger, which we understood, and made clear we understood. To hear us say, "It's sad and wrong that you weren't able to be with her" made Jane feel understood. The last thing a griever needs is to be told they shouldn't feel a feeling.

Grievers need people they can be honest with, people who are safe.

Hug your grieving friends by encouraging them to share their feelings with phrases that invite comfortable responses, such as "You must feel so many different feelings, would it help to share any of them?" At all costs, please avoid, "You really don't mean that," or "You shouldn't feel that way."

Hug with understanding Grief is unpredictable, confusing, maddening, and much more under normal circumstances. Grieving during a pandemic is enough to unhinge the most balanced person. When Amy died, it felt like the world slid off its axis and everything was wrong. During a pandemic, everybody struggles with the world feeling off and out of control. We feel more helpless when faced with the reality that we don't have as much control in life as we thought.

"When the world is out of control, we want to control something. Anything," I said to Tracey. "When Amy died, I needed something to work, so I reorganized my spices." Tracey laughed. I wonder what she has tried to control since then.

Hug with permission "It's okay to not be okay," is a phrase I've repeated to many grievers. Someone said that to me after Amy died and those few words did wonders by giving me permission to be real, to not pretend. It's normal for people to ask how you are doing, but after a loved one dies, it's a question that can make your brain freeze. I suggest something I heard a speaker say, "On a scale of 1-10, I'm about a three (or whatever) today, hoping for better tomorrow." That was a non-emotional answer and protected me from letting words fly, and saying something like, "How the hell do you think I'm doing? My daughter died!"

Hug with preparation The pressures, challenges and uncertainties of the pandemic put enormous strain on courtesy and kindness, and many people react by saying things they wouldn't normally say. Even without a pandemic, people try to say something supportive to those mourning a death, but often end up uttering words that hurt more than help. I try to warn grievers to be prepared, that minds get muddled and mouths get clumsy.

"I'm so glad I'm not you," a friend recalled someone saying to him after the death of his son. My friend was shocked, but apparently so was the one who said that. I encourage grievers to try to be gracious when this happens, and to not take such comments personally. If a griever is dumbstruck by an unfortunate hurtful comment, he or she can simply excuse himself and leave.

I also warn grievers that some of the people they thought would be there for them can't be, because they haven't experienced loss, or haven't dealt with their own past grief. I encourage grievers to be tolerant if possible. They don't know what to do or say, or, as my husband, Jon, says, "They haven't developed the skill." I would add, they haven't *yet*. No one is immune from grief.

Hug creatively Hug with a memory or photo to share if you can. A friend of Amy's put together a book of photos and stories that people sent to a website honoring her. I was thankful for every picture and every memory. I looked at them repeatedly because there would be no new photos taken. No new memories made. This kind of hug is especially meaningful during a pandemic since friends and family can't gather in the same way.

Share time, talents, or resources to reach out and offer support to grievers. I am a writer and helped a friend write her husband's obituary. A friend let me know her college-aged niece felt like a prisoner when she had to isolate in a Super 8 Motel for ten days after testing positive for COVID. She was lonely and far from home and separated from her college friends. I sent a note and then emailed a riddle or corny joke daily. Perhaps you can offer to wash a griever's car or pay a handyman to fix a gate. I've texted others when I'm headed to the market to see if I can pick up groceries for them. Marketing during a pandemic is challenging on its own, but marketing while grieving is so arduous, it often gets postponed repeatedly.

Hug with a gift There are many creative possibilities to honor the one who died, such as starting up or contributing to scholarships, planting trees, donating to charities, making a tribute donation to something meaningful to the deceased, and wearing bracelets or pins with the name of the loved one who died.

I've spoken to many grievers who regret not saying or doing certain things for their loved ones before they died. I suggest honoring their loved one by doing something extra for someone else they might not have done otherwise. It's a kind of second chance.

Hug with words of hope "You will see color again," I said to a neighbor whose son died. "The world won't always look so black and bleak." The world during early days of grief seems dark, more so during a pandemic. Grievers often wear the heaviness of their hearts with slumped shoulders and sluggish steps. I remind them the debilitating pain won't always cover everything. Their steps will get lighter. I couldn't brush my teeth at first without missing Amy, but normal routines do, in time, become more normal again. I remind grievers not to feel guilty when they laugh, enjoy something, or realize they've gone a longer period of time without intense sadness. I tell them it means they are learning to embrace both pain and joy at the same time, learning how to live with grief.

Hug with a nod to the future Pandemics don't last forever. And while grievers will always miss their loved one, their loss doesn't have to define them or keep them from enjoying life again. Loved ones would want us to honor them by living full and meaningful lives, while still remembering them, and loving them.

As time goes on and the pain isn't so debilitating, help grievers get past the emotional hump of thinking the best years of life are over because their loved one is gone. Help plan an outing or shared class or experience in the near future. Suggest a new hobby, and perhaps offer to try it with them. Encourage them to talk about possible trips they might take.

These distance hugs may lack physical touch, but they touch grievers in ways to help them open their arms, open their eyes, and open their hearts to the future.

Granddaughter Mary only missed her mom overnight, but during that time, she needed hugs and love. I will miss Amy for all time, as will all those who grieve, pandemic or not. However, during a pandemic, it is all the more important to find creative ways to reach out and hug each other.

A-VAX

Angela Cybulski

12/28/32

Babe,

Hoping you won't mind email. This place has no service—solid brick, like a bunker, or at least that's how it feels. I think it used to be a prison in the way back—and they took my phone.

Anyway, I'm alright. Got me my own "cell". It's not much, but it definitely ain't prison. I got the basics, but I also have a computer and a shelf of a few books and looks like maybe Netflix. Still need to check that out. They told me I could email and also that they took care of letting you know what I signed up for, had you sign all the waivers and stuff.

I hope you don't mind me not talking this over with you, but they really didn't give me a chance. The protest was off the hook out of hand. I know, I know. I probably shouldn't have gone with Ian and those guys, but I thought it was cool and I could handle myself. And I did. It was just one of those wrong place, wrong time things. It doesn't matter now. They picked up about 100 of us, booked us right there on the street. And some guy in a suit followed up on the booking officer and said we were cleared to make a deal—we could go with him and participate in a trial program to test an alternative option to the vaccine

– in exchange the booking would be reversed – or we could wait for the wagon to take us to county and go that route. Man, I took the a-vax option. Those guys that shot that pro-vaxxer, I mean I wasn't involved, but I was right there. It was messed up. I don't want to get mixed up in anything at county, especially now.

I thought everyone would take the offer, but only me and four other guys agreed. They put us in a black car and brought us a ways out from KC. Tbh, it was black as f*#@ when we came out here and I have no idea where we are.

Listen babe, I'm gonna turn in for tonight. I'll write more tomorrow. Please don't worry about me. I love you and I hope to God you understand why I'm doing this. I wish I could have talked to you first. But sometimes a man just has to choose. Give Nala a kiss from her pop and tell her I'll be home soon. See you on the other side, baby.

Leon

Digital voice report of Dr. James Kushner, Clinical Director, GenoVi Cybertechnologies

Anecdotal Observations: Leon Armignon, Day 1/3

Mr. Armingnon [Mr. A] seemed to settle in well to the conditions here. He has accepted the protocol without question: turned in his mobile device, exchanged his civilian attire for the blue utility jumpsuit, and calmly entered his private domicile. There are 5 cell blocks on the second floor of this building, the 6th is requisitioned for the night guard. Mr. Armingnon's cell is adjacent to the night guard. I noted a slight disturbance when he handed in his mobile device, a flinching on the right-side cheek and eye. However, he is docile and appears resigned to what he has agreed to in good faith. I see no prospective issues with this subject. He is affable and appears to be in tune with the needs of others, evidenced by his assisting one of the other subjects who reacted emotionally to the loss of his mobile device. The man has a terminally ill spouse at home, and he has agreed to participate in this study in an effort to spare her the adverse effects of the mandatory vaccine which he believes would likely end her life even more prematurely. Mr. A assured this subject of the noble work they were entering on and how it would help his wife, but reminded him they would need to make sacrifices. This sort of altruism is exactly what the program is looking for in its test subjects. It is unfortunate we are unable to utilize his skills for a mass marketing campaign. Perhaps excision of portions of his email correspondence to his wife can be used as "after-the-fact" testimonial of the efficacy of the program in the media campaign to steer the anti-vaxxer population to compliance. Mr. A's altruistic manner should in no way lull operatives into a false sense that he is harmless: he is physically robust and appears to be possessed of great strength as evidenced by his body composition and height, carriage and watchfulness. Mr. A has adjusted nicely to his domicile and was observed by me on my 9pm rounds finishing an email to his wife and settling in to read Plato's Republic.

12/29/32

Hey Babe,

Great news! I spoke to the psychologist here today. Nice lady, well, at least she seems so. Ramona Berkley, Dr. Berkley. She's younger than us, but she has a girl, too. Also, three, just like Nala.

Mostly she asked me about why I'm against vaccination for the virus, my values and beliefs and whatnot. I know they're not supposed to take sides, right? I mean, I'm sure she works for this place, or whoever is organizing this thing. But she seemed genuinely interested and concerned for our reasons and values. I explained to her that Nala lost her sight after getting the vaccine for the last virus, and that you lost Jared . . . I told her there's no way a safe vaccine could be developed in a month's time and that we weren't going to tolerate being guinea pigs so people with more power and money could live at our expense. I'm so used to getting attacked for speaking out, and you know I'm super careful of talking about our kids, but she said this project was developed specifically with our concerns in mind and that they really are trying to find a solution that can benefit everyone. She said the government hired the group she works for, I think she said it's called GenoVi, after the last vaccine fiasco and they realize that some of us are going to be resistant to going through another mass vaccination without any clinical trials, so they got out in front of it and phased in a plan for anti-vaxxers. After all the crazy hate-speech out there, it was nice to hear someone speak sanely. Kindly, even.

Anyway, I found out a little more about their plan for anti-vaxxers and I think you'll be impressed. It's a little extreme, and complicated, but represents zero health threat. Basically, they are forming communal pods—people will live in community with other anti-vaxxers in a quarantine-like setting, I guess a little like what I'm doing here, but less restrictive. Not like we'll be living in prison or anything, but just set apart as communities in remote areas and kept safe to reduce the spread and mitigate deaths. She couldn't tell me all the details now, but she said based on what I told her we were excellent candidates for the program. It will be a commitment. The fatality rate without mass vaccinations is calculated at about 90%. I don't know. That lesser of two evils thing may be at play here. But I'm willing to hear what they have to say. If we meet the requirements, you and I can discuss what we want to do when I get home. Should be in a few days' time. She said something about adaptability tests for me and the other guys here tomorrow, so I'll let you know what that's about.

It's about time to eat here. They have us 6 feet apart in what looks like it used to be a mess hall. Food's there on trays when we walk in and I don't see another person except the guys I'm in here with. They kinda been keeping to themselves. Food's alright, I guess. What you'd expect from "prison fare" haha. Last night was Salisbury steak and mashed potatoes and those nasty peas and carrots. Reminds me of when I was a kid. I love you so much and would kill to be eating anything frozen at home with you. See you on the other side,

Leon

Digital voice report of Dr. James Kushner, Clinical Director, GenoVi Cybertechnologies
Anecdotal Observations: Leon Armignon, Day 2/3

Mr. A continues to behave in an exceptional manner. His lack of anxiety, calm demeanor, and relaxed behavior in his cell block must be noted as in no way representative of the mass population and their possible reactions to the Phase 2 (B) protocol. If anything, Mr. A can be considered a research anomaly. Our job is easier, but he provides little by way of red flags for crowd control, mental health contingencies, and resistance mindsets. The other clinicians are getting abundant data on those qualifiers. He does, however, pose a valuable study for the segment of the population who still believes in democratic ideals and in the basic goodness and decency of the human person, regardless of differences. The video feeds from his cellblock, the dining hall, and recreation areas will provide essential material for studying the ways we can marshal the unique qualities of individuals like Mr. A.

to further the cause. An example is his interaction with another young subject named Carl. Carl is an African American, 18 years of age, who lost his mother in the last vaccine campaign. His presence at the protest was intended towards violence. Mr. A has spent time talking with Carl, has calmed him, assured him his participation in the project is a noble effort in memory of his mother and even engaged him in prayer. Carl's demeanor and interaction with the other men in the group has significantly altered since encountering Mr. A. Most notably, he has gone out of his way to attend to Mr. R, the man whose wife is ill at home. The anxiety displayed by all of the participants, the short tempers, the inability to relax, is not apparent in Mr. A. He is even-tempered and truly seems to believe in what he has committed to, and is possessed of a level of trust and optimism missing from the others. He is cautious, however, and practical. Resigned, perhaps. Upon hearing news that his mobile device would be restored to him within 24 hours he looked puzzled and questioned why. It was explained to him that a satellite had been affixed to the roof of the building to access the signal. He appeared to accept the explanation. Mr. A is reading quietly in his cell again at 9pm . . . Plato's Republic.

12/30/33

Babe,

Gonna keep this short. I'm not too sure why I haven't heard from you, but I'm going to assume you're getting these emails.

Just wanted to let you know that I'll be able to call you later on today! A crew here was able to re-orient the satellites and cell service should be up and running this afternoon! I can't wait to hear your voice. If I can call before Nala goes down for her nap, maybe you can put her on, too.

I was told we'd be here at least another 5-7 days, which seems like an eternity, but I can hold out. If they can pull this thing off it will be the answer to everything. The community pod we'll be assigned to is not far from here, according to Dr. Kushner. He met with me today to assess my physical stamina. Sounds like I'm going to be given a job in security at the community pod site! I guess he saw me working the weights in the yard yesterday... See, baby I told you these muscles weren't just for show. (wink, wink)

Anyway, I'll save the rest for when we talk. I promised Carl I'd pray with him before he calls to talk to his family. This kid is so angry but has so much pride and potential. He told me it was his cousin who shot that pro-vaxxer at the protest. So young, guess he's going to get sent up since he didn't have the option to come here. I'd like for you to meet Carl. Pretty sure he'd remind you of some your students. There will be a lot of good we can do if all this works out. This is our chance to stand up, baby. We need to be the change we want to see and support these good efforts. No more violence. I love you. See you on the other side,

Leon

Digital voice report of Dr. James Kushner, Clinical Director, GenoVi Cybertechnologies

Anecdotal Observations: Leon Armignon, Day 3/3

All of the men have been released from their cells into the recreation room to ensure a natural setting and provide clear observation among clinical staff. Mr. A. sat for some time with Carl, talking and praying. His manner is calm, and his mood is generous and enthusiastic. He appears to be looking forward to the phone call to his wife, based on his earlier email. The men have just been given their mobile devices. Mr. A was instructed not to text or use the device in any way until the green light on the wall by the door was lit and the buzzer indicated 1500 hours. The men received this instruction together in a group. Carl reacted angrily to being told he could not use his device and Mr. A helped to quiet him. He pointed out that after three days another 15 minutes wasn't so long to wait. Carl shrugged but appeared to agree and pocketed his device. Mr. A. clapped him on the back. He then went to Mr. R and asked after his welfare. Mr. R indicated he was nervous to call his wife in case her health had worsened. He expressed concern that he had not received any emails. He became agitated and frantic and Mr. A offered to sit with him until it was time to call. Mr. R was grateful, and the two men walked to the sofa near the window and sat down together to wait. Mr. A tried to calm Mr. R by asking him to think of ways he could reassure his wife when he did talk to her. The other three men have sought a space apart, presumably for privacy.

Test protocol set to initiate in 5, 4, 3, 2, 1 . . . The green light has been given. At the sound of the buzzer Mr. R rose rapidly from the sofa and walked away, punching numbers intensely into his phone. Mr. A remained on the sofa and watched Mr. R for a moment. Mr. A is now calmly making his call.

I am switching over to mobile phone interception and interface recording:

(Mr. A's voice) "Hey, baby! It's me! Didn't you get my email? They returned our phones and …"

Mr. A. has ceased speaking and has fallen back on the couch. His arm has fallen at his side and the phone has slipped out of his hand onto the floor. A darkening shadow is observed growing around his nose. This looks to be blood, and suggests the electromagnetic pulse was successful in initiating the aneurysm. Based upon my preliminary observation, extermination of subject is complete.

Psychopomp
Amelia Dellos

It was another Wednesday, and Nurse Diwata continued to run against the morning tide, caring for her patients. Wearing head-to-toe personal protective equipment felt like working in sopping wet clothes. She willed herself to work through the exhaustion. She knew she could do it. A few years ago, during an appendicitis attack, the stubborn nurse worked an entire shift. There were too many patients to treat and not enough minutes in the day.

And to make matters worse, there was a new patient in "The Room." All the nurses hated room 1313. It wasn't just the number thirteen. She wasn't superstitious like that. All the employees knew funky stuff went down there. If Nurse Diwata hadn't witnessed it with her own eyes, she would've dismissed it all out of hand. But she had seen it.

To this day, the nurses still talk about the time her patient, Mr. Malcolm, kept buzzing the call button even after he died. He was a frequent flyer on the floor and his penchant for calling the nurses for anything, even a Kleenex, didn't endear him. When the room was empty, and the call button continued to go off, they all knew without a question who it was. Their old friend Mr. Malcolm.

As a third-generation Filipino nurse, Diwata called her grandmother, her Lola, for advice. "Dia, your name Diwata means 'goddess guarding the spirits.' You must tell Mr. Malcolm his business here on this earth is done. He can no longer stay. It's time for him to leave. Now," Lola told her.

Eventually, the nurses complained so much that the administrators turned the room into storage. Those were the days before COVID-19. Now they needed the space. Spirits and hauntings be damned.

Nurse Diwata stood at the foot of the hospital bed in room 1313. On the other side of the room, she noticed an empty bed summoning her to rest her weary bones. Her head pounded like it was going to burst open. She needed to find some aspirin. But first, caring for her patient was her priority. Aspirin and rest would have to wait.

The patient was so fragile, with ropey veins, brittle bones, and crinkled skin. Another octogenarian transferred to the hospital from a nursing home. Even through Diwata's mask and face shield, the smell hit her like a hard rain.

"I'm Nurse Diwata," she said, in a loud but comforting tone. Her daughter called it her "nurse voice."

"What?" the patient yelled.

"I am Nurse Diwata."

"Do you have a name an old lady can pronounce?"

"You can call me Nurse Dia."

Laying a frail hand on her chest, "Helena."

Gently turning the patient onto her side, "It's such a lovely name."

"Named after my grandmother. A real beauty in her day." Her words cut short as her body shook from coughing.

When the hacking subsided, Nurse Dia began to gently remove Helena's soiled pajamas, filled with diarrhea, leaving a trail from her back to her ankles. "I don't doubt it."

"This COVID business reminds me of the Spanish Flu, but we can't call it that anymore, can we?"

Needing an extra set of hands to clean Helena, Nurse Dia pressed the call button. If she wasn't careful, she could tear the patient's skin and leave her open to infection. She pressed the call button again. Still, no one came. The nursing assistants were all terrified. Last week, her assistant stood frozen in the hallway and threw supplies into the room, making it clear she wasn't earning enough money to risk her life. No additional troops were coming to help her.

When Nurse Dia looked her patients in their eyes, she saw family. Helena belonged to someone. This woman was a grandmother, someone's Lola. She remembered the first time she had to change her Lola's diaper. The woman remained fierce and robust throughout her life until her body began to break down bit by bit. Eventually Lola was forced to have her granddaughter wipe her bottom like a baby. Diwata, a teenager at the time, didn't care. She loved her Lola and wanted nothing more than to care for her. But her Lola was too proud.

Afterward, her grandmother only allowed Dia's mother to change her diaper.

"In those days, no one talked about it after it all had passed over, and life went back to normal. You know, the Great War had ended, the heaviness of it all, sickness and death," Helena said.

Nurse Dia stopped cleaning her. "Talked about what?"

"The influenza epidemic," Helena replied. "Once my grandmother told me how her son had died. He had just turned seven. Did you know back then they would pick up the dead body, wrap it in a sheet, and toss it in a patrol wagon?"

She picked up Helena's leg and wiped the congealed sick from it. "How awful."

"My grandmother ran outside screaming, 'Let me get a macaroni box!' Back then, macaroni came in these twenty-pound wooden boxes. She couldn't stand the thought of her baby piled in a cart like a sack of potatoes."

"What was his name?" Nurse Dia asked.

"Whose name?"

"The little boy in the pasta box."

"Oh, they called him Bernie, short for Bernard."

As Nurse Dia put a clean hospital gown on Helena, Dr. Madhavi and her flock of interns walked in. The nurse and the doctor hadn't always seen eye-to-eye on how to talk to their patients. The doctor had the bedside manner of a matador trying to tame a bull. Behind her back, the other nurses called her "Dr. Mad Hatter." Not only was it tough enough for women in medicine, she had too much respect for the doctor to call her names. Even with an abysmal bedside manner, the doctor outperformed every physician at Cook County. If Diwata got the virus, she wanted Madhavi to treat her and told the doctor as much.

Dr. Madhavi stopped short at the foot of Helena's bed. "Patient, female, aged 84. Underlying conditions: diabetes and dementia. A week ago, the patient tested positive for COVID-19," the doctor said in a clipped tone through her mask.

Nurse Dia interjected, "The patient's name is Helena." She hated how doctors didn't refer to patients by their names. Dr. Madhavi ignored her.

A timid resident raised her hand, "Why hasn't the patient been intubated?"

Dr. Madhavi read Helena's chart, "We have a 'do not resuscitate' on file from the nursing home. We're waiting on confirmation from the family."

The interns, dressed from head to toe in their PPE, looked like science fiction space explorers landing on Jupiter. Nurse Dia thought every batch of fresh doctors, even under their masks, somehow managed to look younger than the last.

Madhavi, a former military officer, cleared her throat. Even through layers of protective equipment, the doctor managed to be imposing.

"What triage would you assign to this patient?"

None of the interns answered her question.

"We don't have all day. We have five new COVID patients who need immediate care. Now. Anyone?"

Even though their shift had just begun, the newbie doctors were already in the deep end without a life preserver.

"Black," answered Nurse Dia. After working a double shift, she was too tired to play the teaching hospital game.

As though the nurse was invisible, Dr. Madhavi looked right through her. Nurse Dia knew the look: it meant the good doctor would find her later and chew her out. But she didn't care. They were now in a war zone, and every day they were losing the battle.

Dr. Madhavi repeated, "Black." Letting them off the hook wasn't an option. "Let's go through the triage codes."

Radio silence from the interns. Dr. Madhavi pointed at an intern concentrating on her shoes.

"You, Dr. Martin, tell me the codes," pointing at one of the interns.

Dr. Martin looked behind her. Then the hapless intern looked up at the ceiling, expecting the answer to fall from the fluorescent lights.

Finally, another intern spoke up. "Red, life-threatening, needs immediate treatment; yellow, non-life-threatening, needs urgent care; green minimal injuries, can delay treatment; and black, death is imminent, pain management only."

"Excellent Doctor," and without another word, Dr. Madhavi turned away, leading her charges to the next patient.

Helena reached out and grabbed Nurse Dia's hand. "I'm scared, and I don't know why."

The nurse squeezed Helena's hand. "I'll take good care of you."

"Don't bother my daughter. She's so busy with work and her children. I don't want to be a nuisance to her," Helena said, her hands shaking.

If Nurse Dia had a dime for every time one of her elderly patients said this to her, she could've retired by now. What were all these useless sons and daughters so busy doing that they couldn't be bothered to care for their dying parents?

"Close your eyes, try and get some rest," she said, touching her shoulder. "I'll be back to check on you soon."

Breaks were rare. While Nurse Dia peeled off the layers of PPE from her clammy skin, she caught her reflection in the mirror hanging from her locker. Her black bob and brown eyes were always shiny like polished silver. Her yoga teacher always said Dia had "fierce prana." People with strong prana, lifeforce, had a light, a sparkle in their eyes.

But now, the sparkle was gone. The pandemic had ground her down. Her skin tone was ashen. Her bright brown eyes were rimmed with deep dark circles.

Her hands were shaky from the constant adrenaline spikes. When did she last eat? Or drink anything other than black coffee? Diwata remembered something about donated coffee and donuts in the break room. The other nurses and assistants all still hung out there. It was a four-by-four coronavirus petri dish. She decided getting food from the hospital cafe would be a safer bet.

She grabbed a bottle of water and a triple-wrapped turkey sandwich. Diwata found her way to a secret spot outside the hospital's chapel. It was an indoor garden gifted to the hospital by some wealthy family. The plaque read, "The Great Influenza Pandemic of 1918-1919. For the souls lost, may they rest in peace knowing they live in our hearts."

Everyone who worked at Cook County knew the history of the flu pandemic because, at the time, the renovated hospital's three thousand beds were full for months on end. Along with the AIDS crisis, it held the title as one of the worst epidemics Chicago had ever experienced. Until now.

She loved the quiet and tranquil garden. It smelled like spring come to life, earthy wet dirt. There were two wooden benches surrounded by enormous ferns grazing the ceiling. As Nurse Dia sat down, every single muscle in her body throbbed. She unwrapped her sandwich and thought of Helena. A wave of nausea slammed against her insides. She couldn't eat. Surrounded by hissing machines and harried strangers, Helena would die alone in an isolated hospital room. There would be no loved one to comfort her, to hold her hand. A nurse checking her vitals would be the only human touch her patient might receive if they weren't too busy.

Before she realized it, big wet tears were streaming down her face. As a third-generation nurse who had seen her fair share of trauma, she didn't cry on the job. Growing up, no matter what happened, her Lola always knew what to say to make it better. Nurse Dia wanted nothing more than to pick up a phone and call her grandmother. A shiver ran up her spine as she remembered a story her Lola told her before dying.

It was one of the many Filipino myths Lola loved to tell. "Dia, there are spirits—angels—who guide deceased souls to the afterlife. They help ferry them across the river to heaven."

She took some comfort in the idea there might be angels keeping her patients company when their loved ones couldn't. For the life of her, Nurse Dia couldn't remember the name of these spirit guides. Was it psychopath? Psychologist? Psychosurgeon? Exhausted, she could barely remember her own name.

The door to the garden creaked open, and Nurse Dia's heart hitched, "Hello?" Every single hair on her arm stood at attention. She limped to the door with her swollen and sore feet. No one was there. She peeked down the hallway and saw a statuesque woman wearing a crisp white blouse with a lace trim collar, a thick long wool skirt, and boots with high buttons up the back walking away. The nurse hobbled after the stranger.

The hallway went sideways on her, forcing Diwata to inch down the hallway using the walls for support. "Where's your mask? You must wear one."

As Nurse Dia entered Helena's room, room 1313, the lights flickered off, leaving a spotlight over her hospital bed. The mysterious woman was perched next to Helena, holding her hand, and laughing like reunited long lost friends.

"You're not supposed to be here, just hospital staff and patients."

"I once was a patient in this very room," the woman replied. Her melodic voice sounded like a song Diwata once knew and loved.

"This is Olive," said Helena. "She's a good egg."

Nurse Dia pitched forward like a boat in choppy water. Hot and cold, her skin no longer hung on her bones. Instead, it crawled over them.

Olive stood up. "Please let me help you," she said, leading her to the unmade bed. "Time to rest."

"My patients, they're all alone. They need me."

Olive smiled down at her. "They have us."

"Who's us?" Nurse Dia asked as Olive tucked her in.

The question had barely left her lips when a group of men and women appeared. They surrounded the bed dressed in army green post-world war clothing.

"No soul dies alone at Cook County," Olive explained. "Not since the flu pandemic over a hundred years ago, we care for them and ensure they all find their way back home."

"What's happening to me?" Before Diwata's body felt like a heavy meat suit, now it felt like a light, fluffy meringue. Then she witnessed her entire life zoom by her all at once, from looking into her Lola's eyes before she died to looking into her daughter's eyes after her birth. She experienced an explosion of light, and love burst from her chest.

"You're in an in-between, my dear. Not quite alive. Not quite dead. It's my job to help you cross the river," Olive said, taking Diwata's hand. "I'm your guide."

Diwata remembered the name of the spirit guides in Lola's story.

"Psychopomp," she whispered. It was her life. It was her story coming to an end. "You're my psychopomp."

Olive nodded her head and smiled. A halo illuminated Olive's face, blurring out her features.

Now, Nurse Dia could see it all. Holding shock paddles in her hands, Dr. Madhavi's face covered in sweat and tears, standing over Diwata's limp body. The hissing ventilator still pumping air mercilessly into her lifeless lungs.

Olive took Diwata's hand, leading her out of the hospital room.

"Dr. Madhavi, you need to call it," the intern said, looking at the heart monitor's flatline and feeling for a pulse.

Diwata watched them. They were suspended in time, waiting for Dr. Madhavi to call her time of death. No matter the situation, the doctor was always unflappable. Never one to hesitate.

"Your boat awaits, dear one," Olive said, pointing to a small wooden boat with a large white pillow floating in a gentle river. "Your Lola will be there to greet you on the other side."

Diwata stepped into the boat and sat down. As it began to drift down the river, the hospital walls melted away, replaced by shimmering sunbeams.

Clearing her throat, the intern repeated, "Doctor."

Looking up at the wall behind the hospital bed, "6:13 PM," Dr. Madhavi said, her voice cracking.

One's Company, Two's a Crowd

Barbara DeMarco-Barrett

The worst heat wave of the summer settled in, but it was unlike past heat waves. This one was worse and not just because of the pandemic. The Earth was heating up. Fires everywhere, rolling blackouts, the desert hotter than ever. The heat made sleep difficult, no thanks to my air conditioner that sounded like a leaf blower as it threw out tepid air. Other residents here at the converted Placent_a Motel—the "i" had burned out long ago—were also fighting the heat, as evidenced by the pool sign-ups. Not knowing who was contagious, we now had to take turns swimming, and people who never gave the pool a second thought were clamoring for their time in the water.

At two in the morning, I went onto the landing outside my second-floor apartment. Traffic on Placentia Street beyond the parking lot was light for a Saturday night. In pre-pandemic times, after the bars closed and inebriated drivers hit the streets, police cars' carnival lights made me feel somewhat celebratory. Now, everyone stayed home. Police must be bored. Poor them.

But not everyone stayed in. Prowlers and burglars were still busy. Nothing kept *them* in.

This morning my neighbor Carmina called across the courtyard: "Mimi, can you talk?"

I put on my mask and went over.

"A man was looking into windows last night," she said, "but I could not see his face. He wore a mask."

Masks keep you safe from the virus, but they do nothing for nailing bad guys.

"It scared me," she said, adjusting the elastic around her ears. Her mask had big red embroidered flowers against a turquoise background.

I leaned on the railing in front of her apartment, watching her kids frolic in the pool.

"It's so risky," I said, "to go looking into windows, with such close quarters and all."

I gestured about. A u-shaped two-story construction built in the '50s, eight apartments plus the manager's quarters, huddled around a swimming pool that had never been cleaner. The sparkling water must have puzzled the birds that had grown used to its murky depths. A small white board hung in the kumquat tree where residents signed up for swim times and took turns. Since March 18, when Orange Countians were ordered to shelter-in-place, the swimming pool had become vital. Residents chipped in whatever money they could to hire a pool cleaner so we could get some exercise and the children could expel bottled up energy. My boyfriend Wyatt, a swimmer, chipped in the most money. He has a generous heart and likes to help.

Now, in the middle of the night, I would've jumped in to cool off, but Jesús, the manager, had turned off the light at midnight. I hoped, because it was a Friday, he would leave it on. More than five months since lockdown, we needed escape hatches at all hours. But no. Jesús had his routine.

I sat on my little stool and lit a clove cigarette. All the lights of the compound were off. I liked this because it allowed me to stay hidden and watch the goings-on, which was usually a lot of nothing. Someone lugging a case of beer up the steps. A couple staggering from their Uber. Barry Manilow issuing from an apartment, crooning for all the ladies who had no idea he was gay, or didn't care.

Right after I thought, *nothing much happens around here*, a figure wearing a baseball cap and a mask strolled in, went to the ground floor corner apartment, and peered in, hands clasped behind his back as if he were window shopping. I gasped involuntarily, drew on my cigarette, my hand shadowing the orange coal to prevent myself from being seen, and put it out. I eased up from the stool so it wouldn't creak, but I must have made a noise because the peeper looked up, saw me, and ran off.

Damn.

I was tempted to run after him—my sister had a prowler who broke in and attacked her—but by the time I made it downstairs, he'd be long gone. I lit back up and paced about, pissed off that someone was prowling around my home base in the dark.

I smoked it down to the filter, then went inside and fell asleep on the couch to the old classic film, *The Big Heat*, apropos viewing, for the weather that had made a bad situation worse.

The following morning, I ran into Carmina in the laundry room. Sweat from the ninety-five-degree heat glued the masks to our faces. I should have planned better and done my wash when I learned of the impending heat wave. Wyatt claimed I've never been good at planning.

"That's how I ended up with you instead of a rich guy," I had teased.

I clicked the washer setting to cold, wishing I could shrink down and jump in with my clothes, then I said, "I saw him."

"When?" Carmina spritzed herself with a little spray bottle attached to a tiny plastic fan that whirled around.

"Last night he was looking into the window of the corner apartment downstairs."

"New lady lives there. Curly red hair. *Muy bonita*. She does hair."

One's Company, Two's a Crowd

I held a clump of my hair that reached down my back, almost to my waist, and studied the ends. "I could use a trim." A haircut would give me a reason to talk to her.

"Maybe someone on the way home from the Tiki Bar?" she said and moved her wet clothes to a dryer, inserting two quarters.

"And what—forgot where he lived?"

Carmina shrugged. "No," she said. "It's not right."

"I don't like it," I said, pouring in soap.

"I will make you gazpacho. It's good on hot days. Cools you down."

That night Wyatt came over for dinner. He was still in his work uniform: gray tee shirt, gray shorts. He delivers furniture, an essential business, so says our governor. He lives alone and when he's not with me, he doesn't see anyone else. On the job he wears a mask, so we assume—hope—we're safe. Who knows?

He came in the door and I said, "Wash your hands," and he sing-songed, "I know," making the word "know" skim board the sound waves for a moment. He went straight to the bathroom sink and the faucet ran too long.

"They're clean already," I called. A Pieces, he loved water.

I stood by the front door when he emerged.

"What're you looking at?" he said.

"There was a prowler last night."

"Here?"

I pointed in the direction of the downstairs apartment.

Wyatt wrapped his arms around me and pressed into me from behind. "I'll peep on you anytime."

"Not funny," I said.

"It's probably just an old boyfriend who wants back in."

"Just?"

"I don't mean it like that."

His breath was sweet on my neck, a mixture of bubble gum and Mountain Dew.

"That's a creepy way to go about it," I said.

"Not everyone has my manners," he said. "I'd ring the doorbell."

As it grew dark, a faint breeze swept into the apartment. Wyatt opened a couple of cold beers and handed me a bottle. I guzzled. More than one and my inhibitions go right out the window.

"It's so hot," I said, and pulled off my tank top, flung it down the hallway in the direction of the hamper, and asked Wyatt to do the same. From all that furniture moving, his six-pack was coming along quite nicely.

Wyatt had to get up early for work. I couldn't sleep. Alcohol and the pandemic didn't help. I went out on the landing and lit up a smoke. A few apartments on the second level still had lights on. Not so much on the ground floor.

I stubbed out the butt and was about to go back inside when the jerk reappeared. A short stocky guy. He hung around the same apartment, peeped in the windows, but didn't try to see if any were open. Didn't try the door. The beer gave me courage. I crept down the stairs. I was going to catch the sucker. I didn't know what I would do when I got him, but I took off, moved as stealthily as I could. I hit the bottom step of the laminate stairway and was rounding the pool when I slipped on a Styrofoam noodle and yelped. The dude heard me and disappeared around the apartment building. Once again, out of luck.

The next morning after Wyatt left, I was out on the landing with my coffee when the red-haired woman in the corner apartment went outside, pulling a chair behind her. She brought out a little cart on wheels with haircutting implements, tied a scarf around her head to hold up her red curls.

Moments later a young man or woman, I couldn't tell which, moseyed up and sat on the stool. S/he wore a mask, as did the stylist, who also wore high heels. She shaved the side of her client's head while the other side remained an inch or two long. Clipped the hair at their neck, was paid, and the customer left.

This went on for the next two hours, during which time I made a fruit salad, smoked three cigarettes, and wondered what the heck was going on with the peeper. Maybe one of her clients had become obsessed with her. She *was* pretty, at least from a distance. It was time to take a stroll.

I went down and introduced myself. "I'm Mimi," I said. "I live upstairs in eleven." I pointed.

She said her name was Holly Maguire and she cut hair outside because the salon where she worked closed down. I said I needed a trim and she said, "What about now?"

Now was fine.

As Holly trimmed my ends in the blazing September heat, I said, "Someone was hanging around last night, looking in your window."

Her scissors stopped moving.

"My window?" she said, sounding stricken.

"The night before, too. Didn't look like he was trying to get in, but he definitely wanted to see in. We had a peeper around here a couple years ago. Maybe he's back."

"Shit," she said and jabbed me with the scissors.

"Ouch." My hand shot up to my wound. I examined my fingers. No blood.

"I'm so sorry," she said. "Maybe it was my ex. It was a bad relationship. I moved here to start over."

"We've all been there," I rubbed my neck.

"I'm a loner now. What with the restrictions loosening up, I go out some, but I never bring anybody home. I'm done. Oh, God, if it was my ex...." She paced about, her red strappy stilettos clicking against the pavement.

Maybe I shouldn't have told her.

"This world is so crazy," she said. "When will this damn pandemic end?"

She wasn't asking as much as she was pleading. She handed me a mirror and said, "I guess this doesn't help you see the back, but it looks good."

She said she was fine with cash, so I paid her, said I was glad we met, and went on my way. She seemed troubled about something, probably her ex. I couldn't put my finger on it. Something embarrassed her. I didn't know her well enough to ask what.

That night I was in my usual spot on the landing, smoking a butt, waiting, but it's like that old saying, a watched pot never boils. The peeper didn't show up. Wyatt was delivering furniture in Arizona and probably wouldn't be by. Around midnight, I went in and was at my kitchen table paging through an *Audubon* magazine, imagining being a crow and flying away from here, when I heard the squeak of footsteps on the landing. Maybe Wyatt finished early and made it by. I peeked through the blinds and my eyes met the eyes of the owner of the squeaky shoes. I gasped, he backed off. I jumped up and ran to the door. Lock it or run after the creep? I ran onto the landing, but he was already on the ground floor, powering past the pool.

Wyatt came by the next evening for dinner. Since the pandemic, gone were our dinners out, such as they were—the local taco place or vegan restaurant. Still, we got to be together.

When he came in, he could tell something wasn't right.

"What's up, darlin'?" he said.

"The prowler was here."

"Where?"

"Here!"

He shook his head. "That's not good."

"No kidding."

"You call the police?"

"What're they going to do? By the time they arrived, he'd be long gone."

Wyatt nodded, went to the fridge for two beers, and handed me one, not before tapping it with his own.

"The new neighbor gave me a trim yesterday."

"Looks good," he said, squinting at my head. "Turn around."

"Bullshit. You didn't even notice. That's not the point anyway."

"I noticed," he said, in a little I'm-sensitive-to-you voice. He pulled me to him, picked up a horse tails-worth of my long hair, and studied it.

I took my hair back and said, frowning, "Something is off. I'm worried about her. And the creep wandering about. What if he's dangerous?"

"Oh, no," he said. "The last time you worried about someone, you almost got yourself arrested."

"What—would you prefer I ignored people in trouble? Is that what you'd like?"

"Actually, yes," he said. "I would like that very much."

"Sorry, you got yourself the wrong girl."

"How come you won't let *me* call you girl?"

"Woman, girl, whatever. Something is wrong."

"Let's enjoy our night," he said. "Worry later."

In my galley kitchen we made bean tacos and a green salad. We sat on the landing and ate, a respite from the apartment that had warmed up from all the cooking. A breeze stirred. We watched the kids in the pool below and enjoyed the violet sky as the sun died away. Holly's apartment remained dark. There was no way to know if she was in there or if she'd gone out.

Wyatt and I finished off a bottle of chardonnay when he said, "It's so hot. I feel like taking a swim."

"Kids got the pool," I said.

"Feel like a shower?"

"Let's."

Afterward, Wyatt went to bed—he'd been driving all day. I pulled on a sundress and went out on the landing with my smokes. I listened to podcasts, watched YouTube videos on my phone. Time melted.

It was after midnight when the stalker returned. The hair on my arms and neck stood up. I was ready for him. The door opened from the inside of Holly's apartment and he walked right in. A light went on inside and vague blue shadows played on the walls. Maybe the TV. I remembered she'd said she would not bring anyone inside, so what was up with that?

I grabbed my phone and put on my mask. If I had to go downstairs, I wanted to be ready. As I came out, I heard something break. There was movement inside Holly's apartment. Someone yelled and I didn't have to think about it, I went on alert. Shapes were moving in there. Must be the same stocky guy as before, the one who'd been creeping about. I ran downstairs and as I did, I saw the dude hitting Holly with an object. As I grew closer, I saw he was bludgeoning her with the red stilettos she wore when she cut hair.

I ran inside, hefted a ceramic sculpture that sat on a shelf by the door, and knocked him upside the head. He called out, a rather feminine tone to his voice, and crumpled onto Holly's carpet. Holly began crying. What a great night for Wyatt to turn in early, damn him.

The dude splayed out as I called 911. He was out cold. Soon the sirens were upon us, which brought some of the residents outside. They watched from behind masks.

The EMTs rushed in. One said, "What happened?" and I told her.

Another pulled off the dude's mask and revealed not a dude but a dudette. I looked at Holly.

"My girlfriend," she said. "Didn't like that I left her, but she had this awful temper." Her voice trailed off.

"I can see that," I said.

"Girls beat up girls all the time," Holly said. "You'd be surprised."

"Not much surprises me anymore."

The police arrived and took my statement and Holly's just as Wyatt walked up to us and nodded at Holly.

The policewoman said I could go.

As we went back upstairs, Wyatt said, "You were right again."

"What can I say?"

We crawled into bed. Wyatt pulled me to him, and we fell asleep like that, sweaty and close.

Legacy

Anne Dunham

Olivia's stomach dropped when her aunt Jayne pulled a crumpled envelope from the kitchen drawer. She shrugged and held her aunt's troubled gaze. Addressed to Olivia, the letter didn't have a return address, but she recognized the cursive handwriting that graced at least a dozen letters she refused to open.

"You rifled through my trash?" Olivia asked, and immediately felt sorry for the accusation.

They stood at the kitchen counter. The expansive marble-topped island separated the kitchen from the rest of the house. Afternoon sun slatted through the line of shuttered windows and French doors that led to the backyard patio. Hard-edged shadows from the late autumn afternoon fell on the pine floors. Olivia always imagined the long shadows as swords. As though the afternoon stormed the house in an offensive maneuver.

"It was in the trash bin outside." Her aunt shifted her weight and said, "He is being paroled in a few months."

"Maybe not?" Olivia said with all the deadpan she could muster. She sat at the counter. Her tall frame lowered onto a stool placed her at eye-level with her aunt. "Besides, isn't there a halfway house stint before he's really free?"

Her aunt sat and her soft midsection rounded under her gray t-shirt. She placed her forearms on the countertop and clasped her hands on the counter. A lock of her blonde bob fell in front of her eyes.

Olivia caressed the three healed hash cuts on her arm. She watched as her aunt's eyes moved from her scars to the marble countertop, as though the long gray striations held a secret code that could solve all the strife from past years. Fine lines softened the skin around her aunt's eyes and mouth. Though her aunt rarely lost her composure, Olivia wondered if she pushed Aunt Jayne beyond the limits of her own self-control. Regret needled her. The light in the room darkened. Olivia sat on her hands as a preemptive measure. She sensed her aunt might reach out and touch her.

"We've talked how grudges will only harm your progress," her aunt said.

"He killed her." Olivia raised her eyes to meet her aunt's pale blue eyes. Identical to her mother's and hers.

"She contracted COVID while in the hospital." Her aunt sighed as though she had repeated this fact to the point of exhaustion. "We don't know if she would have lived."

Olivia pause a moment. She turned seventeen a week ago, celebrated by an intimate dinner with her aunt and two older cousins, her aunt's sons. Like any other dinner of the week except the dessert was a homemade nine-inch square vanilla cake with chocolate frosting and two candles in the shape of numbers. Without her mother, she felt on the periphery. She craved to fit in with her aunt and cousins. Bereft of friends, she yearned to fit in anywhere.

Three years earlier a car accident caused a mild brain injury, limiting her emotional language to a range between numbness and anger. Over time she learned to recognize and manage the triggers that sent her into a blinding rage. As time wore on, the grief for her former life started to undermine healing. During the meal, she feigned the signs of what she believed a teen her age would demonstrate. Delight and happiness. The family embraced her as one of their own, and in return all she could offer were hollow gestures, like fake smiles.

Even now, three years after the accident, she couldn't recall much about the night her dad drove her mom and her home from a restaurant, drunk. He lost control of their car on that rainy night and careened off the road. The only traces leftover from that night were the panic and terror seared into her memory before the seat belt failed. She flew through the front windshield. Two weeks later, she awoke from a coma, and her mom was in ICU in critical condition. Her dad pleaded guilty to a third DUI, which he was now serving at a California prison.

Through years of one-on-one and group therapy, she learned the art of mimicking the traits of those not blunted by trauma. She studied people who, through some form of alchemy, could telegraph emotions into genuine and outward expressions. During the birthday dinner, her insides brittle with doubt and self-judgement, she smiled and laughed with her family.

Olivia blinked at her aunt. The familiar shudder in her ribcage started to hum. She squeezed her eyes shut and measured her breaths to stop anger rising. Once in her neutral place she opened her eyes.

"Oli, there is so much for you out there." Aunt Jayne stood and picked up the envelope. "Continue with online classes or we can find a way for you to live away at college. "This," she held up the letter, "is a step towards the latter."

Olivia's frustration throbbed in her head. Her ritual of baiting her aunt seemed to short-circuit her progress. A pain shot into her neck muscles. Damn, she chastised herself. She rubbed her neck. Self-sabotage is what her therapist, Dr. Jan, called this type of behavior. Her aunt's suggestion to attend college seemed out of reach for her. Her brain's limitations controlled the pace of her day-to-day progress towards healing. Though she resigned herself to the possibility of a dull existence, the notion of semi-independence glimmered like a mirage on a desolate road.

An idea struck, and she pulled out her phone. "Aunt Jayne." She tapped a few times on the screen and showed it to her aunt. "Dr. Malek texted that a spot opened in her group."

"The teens who lost parents to the virus?" Aunt Jayne peered closer at the screen.

"Yep," Olivia said.

"You didn't seem all that interested." Her aunt's tone was hesitant.

"Dr. Jan said it's good I try different types of groups." Olivia pulled back her phone. "I'll still go to Alateen meetings. But she said…" Her voice faltered.

"What did she say?" Aunt Jayne's brows pulled together.

"If I'm too comfortable with the same group, it can become a crutch. She said change is good." Olivia had grown complacent with the meetings. She spent two years in Alateen and met often with the same support group of teens who coped with alcoholic parents. The meetings helped for a time, but in the past months the desire to move past her current state and be cured became an obsession.

"Okay. Good. She mentioned that group to me and said some kids are showing progress." Her aunt sat again, and nodded approval. "The situation with Claire was so unpredictable."

Olivia held her breath. She refused to accept COVID stole her mom's life. Her dad would always bear the brunt of her wrath, but she nodded anyway. Her Aunt Jayne needed something else to blame for the loss of her sister, though she was wrong.

They discussed the time and location. Olivia convinced her aunt she could get herself to the place by bus.

"I'll be fine. It's at one of the rooms at Hinkley Elementary," Olivia said.

"Glad they are finding some use for those closed schools," her aunt said, as she opened the refrigerator. Her voice trailed off, as though distracted. "Dinner in about an hour."

Olivia grabbed the envelope and crossed the family room, stepping over the shutter's blade shadows. Before she reached the stairs, she stopped at the black baby grand piano. Family photos in different sizes and types of frames lined up in an uneven row. She bent over and studied a photo of herself when she was twelve and had just won a tennis match at the country club to which her parents belonged. Her long brown hair was brushed into a ponytail, and silver braces glinted from her smile. She held a first-place trophy for singles. Her life before she grew into her large knobby knees and fit into a size ten shoe. Gangly athleticism itching to burst forth from a pre-teen body.

Along with stealing her mom away, her father's recklessness cost Olivia a chance at the life she observed in the frame. The naive girl in the picture frame might as well be a stock photo. Olivia felt no compassion for her. Trapped in time, the girl would remain suspended in that moment of eternal joy and pride forever. Olivia wasn't that fortunate. She let a moment of heat wash over her and balled her hand into a fist. Her knuckles tapped against the glass. The picture fell over, but the glass remained intact. The expected glint of satisfaction from her anger failed to surface and instead a pang of guilt sliced through her. She looked over her shoulder. Aunt Jayne was bent over the freezer drawer. Olivia righted the picture. She smoothed her hand over her short platinum hair. Then, she charged up the stairs, taking two steps at a time.

A few days later at dusk, Olivia approached the former elementary school with trepidation. She squinted at the school's low-slung brick façade now blighted with graffiti. Bent and mangled tall chain link fencing surrounded the building. Weeds strangled the overgrown grass on the lawn area, flanking the school's entrance. A gate with a chain and padlock stood open. She made her way to the school's front double doors and winced at the destruction as she walked along the concrete path.

Once the pride of neighborhoods, all public schools had succumbed to COVID's scourge. Three years ago, a virulent second wave hit California fast and hard, killing ten percent of adults over the age of 50. At the time, Olivia recuperated at home from the crash. While she worked on regaining her balance, politicians, in shielding their own inactions, blamed public schools for the spread. Approval from communities swelled in favor to shut down schools. Though Olivia was safe from the virus, her mom, who had been placed in a convalescent home, caught the virus, and died.

Olivia followed the directions on the placards to find the room. Certain the meeting would be held in a multipurpose room, she grew wary as she walked down a long hallway. A sign placed by a doorway indicated the "Surviving COVID" meeting would be held in a classroom. Olivia peeked inside.

Instead of chairs lined up in rows like Alateen meetings, a dozen desks were configured into a circle and sat in the room's center.

"Hello, Olivia?"

She jumped at the voice behind her. A young woman with long red hair and pale freckled skin moved beside her.

"Yes," Olivia said.

"I'm Dr. Malek. Welcome." Dressed in capri jeans and an oversized sweatshirt emblazoned with UCLA's logo, she could be mistaken for someone Olivia's age. A blue denim mask covered the lower part of her face. "Do you have the forms?" she asked.

"Yes." Olivia pulled two forms filled out in longhand from her backpack.

"As you know, masks aren't necessary, but I ask in consideration for those who still wear one, to please do so."

Olivia gripped the black scarf around her neck and pulled it over her nose and mouth.

"Perfect," the doctor said. She stepped inside the room. "We'll start in about ten minutes."

Olivia inched her way into the room. The black outfit she chose; leggings and a long-sleeve tee-shirt wouldn't camouflage her in this seating configuration. Unlike the Alateen meetings, where she hid in the back row, the circle formation encouraged participation. Her black outfit and platinum hair made her a study in high contrast.

As she moved towards the circle, six faces stared at her. All wore masks. Her muscles tensed and a slight quiver rose in her chest. Before she had the chance to retrace her steps, her aunt's push toward a life that resembled her former one, rooted her to the floor.

She inhaled the faint lavender scent she spritzed over the face covering.

Olivia's gaze swept the dull gray plastic bucket seats. The chairs looked closer than the six-foot social distance compliance. Along with a mask mandate, this rule was obsolete since a vaccine wiped out the virus a year ago. Adherence to outdated rules now served as merely a symbolic gesture meant to placate those who suffered from the virus's lingering psychological effects. The virus claimed not only California's older population but created a growing segment of young adults who developed varying degrees of social anxiety.

The former classroom showed signs of quick abandonment. Three tall beige metal shelves still lined the far wall and contained a few stray books. A handful of student work still adorned the walls; a project of their portraits made with construction paper and found household supplies. Dried beans for eyes, pipe cleaner bent into the shape of a smile formed mouths, and different colored yarn in varying lengths gave each of the similar artworks an identity. A sense of wistfulness beset Olivia. At some point she created such a masterpiece, but her mind blurred those memories and she could only fill in blanks with her imagination.

Olivia walked around the circle as though she was in a game of Musical Chairs. She ignored the seats opposite with occupants. All the chairs would fill eventually, but her pulse eased as she hung her backpack onto a chairback with empties on both sides and a vacant chair on the other side of the circle. She debated on whether to use the collapsed writing desk. It would impede a quick getaway, but Olivia felt safer with a barrier between the rest of the participants and herself. She clicked the small wood writing shelf in place.

A male with a shaved head wearing a Batman insignia on a black mask nodded at her. Two blonde girls who looked similar had written their names with a red marker on their masks. Some of the faces had grown bored with her and hunched over their phones. By the time she settled into the chair, all the masked faces, even Batman, were consumed with other distractions.

Olivia looked up to the stare from a guy who had taken a seat opposite her. He leaned back into his chair. Long legs stretched out in front with his arms crossed. She forced herself not to look. Instead of a mask, a tattoo covered the lower part of his face, like Native American war paint. Instead of a solid color, vibrant inks filled the shape, and articulated a design that detailed out his plight. She had not seen one of these people before but heard rumors about a rising faction of Mexican American COVID victims who used their bodies as physical testaments to their suffering and their crime; they had infected family members who died. An interpretation of the Mexican holiday, Día de Muertos, where the culture honors the deceased, these victims' permanent graphic depictions served as a crusade to shock the community and to hold current politicians accountable; because they too, shared guilt.

Olivia's scars tingled under her long sleeve tee-shirt. She gave a furtive glance, not raising her eyes to his, but enough to study the tatts on his exposed skin. Names and dates inked on arms and legs indicated a horrific number of family members he lost. Curiosity led her to continue. Red spots rendered in the likeness of blood clots dotted the area around his neck. Cursive lettering wove words into a tapestry. *Hate and Love. Anger and Forgiveness. Rage and Joy. Bitterness and Pleasure.* Everything that was taken from him, was scrawled into his skin like a declaration to claim a troubled legacy. The name *Alejandro Perez, Sr.* was tatted on his right forearm.

The heat from his stare burned into her. Her eyes met his, still unflinching. Her insides contracted. Her finger drummed the desk. Three breaths brought her back to the familiar numbness, her home base where thoughts didn't get muddled and confused. A newcomer to the group, did she pique his curiosity? An unfamiliar face invading his space.

His desire to shine a light on regrets and misgivings evoked Olivia's sense of loss. She recognized the brazen courage to heal oneself. A few years in Alateen meetings gave her chances to air her grievances against her dad, but she always chickened out. Until recently she resigned herself to living with those consequences.

She squirmed in her chair; an internal heat like a furnace flipped on and agitated the scars on the tender part of her thighs and arms and lower abdomen. Cutting wounds into her skin was not in service to her family, but merely a ploy to feel different pain when life's monotony grew too enormous to endure. Her scars, like so much of her emotional disconnect, hid in the dark. As though her losses would never rise to meet the level of Tatt Man's worthiness, a feeling of shame prickled just beneath her skin. *Alexjandro, Sr.* must be his dad. She wondered if he was a good dad.

A faint smile crossed his face before he placed a simple dust mask on.

A small charge of courage surfaced, and she sensed an ally in his black eyes. Her mood lightened and she felt a tug to respond. Before she acted on it, a girl plopped herself in an empty seat although there were a few open beside her.

"Hey, dude. Saved me a spot, yeah?" Shrink-wrapped in a short black dress, the young woman's sun-browned skin shone against her thick brown mane that cascaded over her shoulders. "Hot today?" She all but burned through the room's oxygen.

From a few feet away, Olivia smelled alcohol.

He nodded once as a sign of recognition and then righted himself in the chair. "Mask?" Without moving, he seemed to shift his weight to one side of the desk.

"Right." Her head tilted to the side, and she giggled before she pulled a mask decorated with daisies from her purse. She looped the elastic over her ears. "How do I look?" she asked while batting her eyelashes. She leaned towards him and bumped elbows. "Yeah?" She turned her attention to Olivia. "Someone new?" Her face animated as though greeting a long-lost friend. She waved.

A vague feeling came over Olivia. Some detail about Shonda's appearance or behavior shook lose an odd sensation. Thick fog obscured her recall, but something tripped her trigger warning. As Olivia tried to dig into her mind's recesses, Batman Mask stood and strode across to Shonda.

"Saved you a seat by me," he said. His defensive tone piqued Olivia's and the others' attention.

"Gerald, please. Take your seat." Dr. Malek didn't miss a beat. Her voice was muffled under the mask.

Batman Mask didn't acknowledge the doctor. Instead, he stood with his arms crossed and said, "C'mon. You promised."

Shonda turned her head towards Tatt Man and rolled her eyes, which seemed to agitate Batman Mask.

"You ignoring me?" Gerald's voice rose in irritation. He grabbed the small writing surface and shook it.

"Gerald, this is inappropriate. Return to your seat, or you'll need to leave." Dr. Malek's moved to Gerald's side.

"Asshole." Shonda recoiled in her chair.

"Dude, back away." Tatt Man stood and wedged himself between Gerald and Shonda, forcing Batman Mask to release the desk. "Give her some space."

Gerald closed the space between Tatt Man.

"Back-up," Tatt Man said. Though he was inches taller than Gerald, he threw up his hands in a defensive motion. His shoulders rounded and he slid into his chair. His breath puffed out his mask. He closed his eyes and placed his forehead on his desk.

"Freak," Gerald said.

"I'm calling your father." Dr. Malek stepped to her chair and grabbed her purse.

Olivia witnessed the skirmish with heightened interest. The verbal altercation rang familiar. She breathed in vain to steady her pulse, but the scene evoked panic like a claw squeezing the air from her lungs.

The others started a chorus imploring Gerald to return to his seat. Dr. Malek raised her hands in an effort to stop the chaos that threatened to derail the meeting.

Gerald glared at Shonda before he stepped backed. He raised both hands as a gesture of surrender. Dr. Malek turned at this moment and he clipped her chin with his shoulder.

A stunned expression crossed the doctor's face, making her appear like a vulnerable teen under attack.

The disruption sparked a hot anger in Olivia. Her vision tunneled and white flashed before her eyes. An invisible force pulled her from her desk and like an undertow, shoved her to the room's center. Her arms extended towards Gerald in a protective reflex.

"What? You and Alex Shonda's bodyguards?" Gerald shook his head. "Don't worry, I'm outta here. Bunch of losers."

Olivia grabbed the front of his t-shirt.

"What the F, dude," Gerald said. "Are you insane?"

"Yeah, I am." Olivia taunted him. "Gonna hit me, big man? Make you feel important to bully someone weaker? C'mon," she said, pointing at her chin.

"You're mental. Leave me alone." Gerald retreated, but Olivia's anger fed her rage, like a match burns kindling.

Olivia's voice erupted into a scream. "You're pathetic, you stupid idiot." She caught a herself, surprised those words tumbled out of her mouth. She clasped both hands over her mask before more expletives escaped.

The room quieted. Olivia felt Dr. Malek at her side, talking in a soothing voice, but a roar in her head obliterated everything. Her heart pounded. In an instant, she was transported to the night of the crash. She lay on a stretcher in the back of an ambulance. The meaty weight of her dad's sweaty hand clasped hers. The bright light edged his dark clothing as he sat crumpled against the ambulance cabin's white walls. He sobbed and whispered her name. His face and hair slick from rain, dripped into a puddle on the floor.

Then a series of images from that night flickered before her, like a broken film reel. Coiled into a fetal position in the back seat, her eyes were shut tight. The noise from that night smothered much of anything. Sirens, EMTs, firefighters and police scrambled through the chaos.

Then Olivia's mind zeroed in on one moment. The memory gave her such a start, she sucked in a sharp breath.

She watched as it played out in slow motion. Before the car flew off the road, her mom, with slurred speech, screamed obscenities at her dad. She turned towards him. Her body strained against the seat belt. She punched him in the face before shoving him hard. The moment froze as the room spun. The words she screamed at Gerald echoed in her head. Musty scent from rain and metallic odor from blood rushed Olivia. She flinched. The room finally came into focus. She articulated voices. Dr. Malek handed her a plastic cup filled with water. Gerald had retreated to his chair.

Olivia spun around and faced Shonda. Though there wasn't any physical resemblance to her mom, the same alcohol trace that wafted from her mom was undeniable. "You. It was always you." Tears welled in her eyes. Exhaustion throbbed in her bones. She wrestled her backpack from the chair and plodded towards the door. Her chest heaved as she tried to suppress a sob. She forced her arm up and without looking back, fanned out her fingers. A tacit goodbye before she exited the room.

Olivia stepped into a moonlit night. A breeze chilled the tears on her face. She waited by the bus stop. Tatt man, or Alex, occupied her thoughts. She envied his courage to make public his responsibility for such tragedy. By some innocent circumstance, he killed those he loved. Olivia couldn't remember the last time she thought of her dad without hate percolating in her gut. Her mother certainly wasn't innocent.

Remorse took hold when she remembered what day it was. The urgent matter spurred her to take off on foot. Her pace quickened as she passed another bus stop. Trash picked up this morning. She pictured the crumpled envelope heaped on a pile of kitchen waste. She prayed her vigilant aunt checked the trash bins again.

Make A Wish

Jennifer Irani

My mom was always hopeful. Despite the heat and the fire in Tahoe, she insisted we walk to the fountain for my birthday. It was our ritual that began when I was old enough to sit on a baby swing and feed the ducks around Virginia Lake. She handed me a Buffalo nickel. "Make a wish." Her voice was bright and cheery through the dust mask. I was hot and uncomfortable in mine.

It was nine in the morning and I was sweating. My thick black bangs stuck to my forehead. Little tornadoes spun dry leaves in circles in the empty playground. They looked like they were chasing each other, like the kids used to do before the temperatures reached 120 degrees and triggered an early fire season.

I held the coin in front of my new t-shirt with the slogan, "There Is No Planet B." I made a wish about Emmitt, my lab partner and crush, and our Azolla fern experiment. The nickel bounced off the side before diving into the stagnant water. The fountain was shut off after years of drought.

"Happy 16th birthday, Maizey. Promise me you'll never forget this day and how much I love you." She reached over to hug me, but I pulled away. Not because I didn't love her. I hated to be touched.

I never felt the need to say *I love you*. Love was like hydrogen and carbon—elements that existed everywhere. It was redundant to say it.

I kept my promise, but under circumstances I would never had wished for.

The Sierra Nevada mountain range rose to the west of our home in Reno. The fire was on the other side of the ridge on the California side of Lake Tahoe. We could not see the smoke. Yet. The mountains were beautiful, from any angle and any time of day, like my mother was. Her long, black hair rippled down her back like the Truckee River at night and her green eyes were the color of pine. The mountains and my mother were timeless. Steady. Consistent and strong.

My mom was a respiratory therapist and my father was a family physician. They hoped I would be a doctor, but when I was seven years old, I declared that I was going to be an Earth Doctor. "I'm going to help Earth breathe like you help people at the hospital." I pressed a stethoscope on my globe and listened for a heartbeat.

The following week, before school got out for summer, Emmitt and I were honored with first place at the National Climate Science Fair for propagating the Azolla fern and modifying it so that it thrived on water and land. One of my wishes had come true.

The day summer began, Emmitt and I got to work.

The unprecedented heat wave and fire fueled our cause. We were excited about a fern that absorbed trillions of tons of carbon dioxide fifty million years ago through its tiny gnat-sized leaves. It was a super-hero plant and we had big plans for it. We watched videos about guerilla gardening on the YouTube channel, SoulPancake, and learned how to make seed bombs. We planted ferns in rows five feet apart in my quarter-acre backyard. We kept notebooks on their growth pattern that increased on hotter days. They doubled in size every two days. The summer heat worked to our advantage. But we needed to plant them soon or they would be too big to carry.

High winds fueled the flames of the Tahoe fire toward Squaw Valley. It burned so hot it scarred the earth and melted the dirt into glass. My science teacher told us that the Tahoe fire was hotter than previous fires and the forest would not be able to regenerate. I hoped she was wrong.

Emmitt and I kept working. We bought kiddie pools and grew more ferns in the water. They grew even faster in water and tripled in size in two days. We were almost ready to plant.

The next day my mom heard about a new virus from a doctor that worked in Tahoe. The patients developed a rash on their fingers and toes, and it could attack the lungs, liver, and heart. The doctors suspected it was spread through animals and jumped to humans when the fires started.

She wore a respirator and face shield when she left for work. Within days, the virus spread to downtown Reno. The governor issued stay-at-home orders. Everything closed overnight.

Emmitt and I researched the virus online. *Scientific American* said climate change and the fires set up a perfect environment for the new virus that thrived in heat. Two events allowed the virus to mutate and become so deadly. The first event was that the virus took advantage of the weakened environment after years of drought and bark beetle infestations. This destroyed animal habitats, which forced them to live closer together, making them more susceptible to illnesses. The second event, and the weirdest thing about the virus, was that it used the animal carcasses as a host, and it seeded and traveled with the smoke and ash.

The virus spread as fast as the fires. My mother said the hospital was overwhelmed and refused to accept patients.

My parents stocked up on emergency food and installed a portable air filtering system in the house. Always hopeful.

Emmitt and I had respirators from our AP chemistry class, and we had a plan. Late at night, when the wind blew the smoke out of Reno, we rode our bikes to the park wearing our respirators and helmets. Our bike baskets were loaded with Azolla ferns and seed bombs. We pedaled along the river to downtown. No one was on the roads. I felt liberated. The moon illuminated the giant plumes of gray and white smoke from the ridge. It was ominous, like a malevolent genie.

We planted in center dividers, vacant fields, and threw seed bombs over fences into construction sites. On our way home, we dropped several ferns on Virginia Lake.

The next day, high winds blew the Tahoe fire over the ridge and it ran down the mountain toward Reno in streams of fiery fingers. Burning confetti fell from the sky and ignited the dry chaparral surrounding the horse ranches near us.

Mom was exhausted from treating patients that flooded into the hospital. Patients sat in hallways. Some died waiting to be seen. She told Dad that it was like a war zone. Nurses and attendants refused to go to work because they did not have enough protective gear. Mom was frustrated about the situation and how unprepared they were. I never saw her get angry before.

The winds blew a thick orange smoke into our neighborhood. The houses across the street disappeared. A fine, gray ash covered our ferns, yard, and cars. My eyes stung and I felt a wheeze in my lungs.

Emmitt and I stopped our planting when the smoke and fires made it too dangerous. We talked over Zoom instead. We both had a bad habit of rubbing the backs of our necks when we were nervous.

"Is the back of your neck as raw as mine is?" I asked him.

"Yep." He forced a laugh. "Hope the ferns survive this." His brown eyes had the same curious spark as when he found a pill bug at recess in first grade. His hair grew out from a fade on the sides with a high Afro on top, to tight curls around his face. He looked good any time of day. I wrote that down in a letter I would give him one day when I had the courage. For now, I stashed it away in my drawer.

"If they can survive for fifty million years, they'll survive this." I doodled in my journal. I wasn't good at small talk and was a little shy.

Emmitt held a drawing up to the camera. "Check this out."

My eyes traced his delicate pencil lines of a hummingbird. "That's beautiful."

When we ran out of things to say we could just vibe. I liked that about us. I put on "Summertime Sadness" by Lana Del Ray. He finished the wings on the bird while I worked on ideas for a poem:

June 7th

Emmitt and I are talking on Zoom now and we are both anxious about the fires and the virus. We don't know how much more the ferns can take. The Sierra Nevada Mountain range turned into a smoldering body that suffered third-degree burns along its spine. It's like Earth caught a virus that was just as deadly as ours was. I miss the smell of the vanilla-scented bark of the Jeffrey Pines that are now carbonized silhouettes. The big blue sky that I love waking up to every day is clouded in yellowish dirty smoke. The red moon glows at night like a large, dusty lens with a giant eye behind it looking at Earth trapped in a petri dish. Was I the scientist or a specimen?

We were the deer that leaped out of the flames only to run into a larger fire.

We stayed up past midnight before saying good night.

The fires and the virus were overwhelming. When I got anxious, I counted things. I stayed up and tallied populations, which freaked me out more: 1.43 billion in China, 1.3 billion in India, and 328 million in the United States. A total of 7.8 billion people populated the world, and everyone needed toilet paper.

The United States used more than seven billion rolls of toilet paper a year, which took 27,000 trees per day to make. I was sure the lady that pushed her cart in front of Mom and loaded up her pick-up truck with TP at Winco Grocery had at least half of that.

I woke up the next morning with a calculator in my hand.

That night my father came home with deep red indents where the mask pressed against his face for twelve hours. His glacier blue eyes were gray and tired.

"We lost two doctors and a nurse." Dad dropped into a chair. I think he was crying. I didn't know what to say to people when they cried. I brought him a glass of water and sat down on the other side of the table.

June 20th

Dad lost three friends today. It didn't have to be this way. If people worked together, we could have avoided all this. That's why I love working with plants. They are symbiotic. Interdependent. They survive by a form of socialism that was biologically necessary. But people aren't so good at that. I hope my parents don't get sick. I'm still crushing on Emmitt. I miss seeing him in the real.

Mom was on night shift. A worried look drained her face on her way out of the front door. A mask hung around her neck, insufficient for the battle she faced like the firefighters holding a hose in front of an inferno the size of a city block.

Dad went to bed. He seemed more tired than usual.

Emmitt and I stayed up and played Minecraft. We invented virtual cities and farms. When we got bored playing games, we pulled up maps of Reno and planned out routes for planting.

The fires shifted into the foothills behind us. Emmitt said it would stop at the Truckee River, but it turned out the fire walked on water. People evacuated from their homes and slept in their cars in parking lots normally used for country fairs and horse shows. Cases of the virus increased as the fire grew larger and more intense.

My parents learned that although most children were immune, they carried high levels of the virus. We were considered super spreaders. I felt like an alien lived inside my body. I kept to my bedroom as much as possible and wore my mask inside the house. I wasn't sure what was worse, the fires or the virus. Both were intolerable and merciless.

The hospital required my parents to test for the virus every morning. But my parents wouldn't get sick. They were first responders. Angels. Protected. Nothing would happen to them. They were careful and they took all the precautions, I told myself. Within a week my father tested positive and isolated himself in the bedroom. Mom placed my potted Azolla ferns near his bed. They would clean the air and Dad would be better soon.

Mom took a week off work to help Dad. By the end of the week, the Azolla ferns were ten times their size, bursting out of the pots. His strength and appetite increased. I couldn't prove it, but I believed the ferns helped Dad get better, along with Mom's love.

The fire exploded overnight and spread into the valley like a flood of water. Waves of flames roared above the trees. Ranchers on the other side of our park evacuated, taking their horses to Fernley. I hoped all the wild mustangs in the hills survived, including the colt that came down to our yard last fall with her mama to eat apples off our tree.

I was extremely anxious about the fires and the virus. My stomach was tender. I couldn't eat. My mind played tricks on me. I heard my Grandma's voice one night telling me everything would be okay.

The news reported that the virus mutated into a more transmissible and deadly version at the same time Mom resumed working.

Her hours at the hospital were long. She worked four twelve-hour shifts in a row. I wished she wasn't considered an essential worker. She was my essential mom. She came home more tired and upset every day.

Mom left me a note on the kitchen counter the following morning: "Dear sweet Maizey, I'm in isolation with your father. Don't worry, I feel fine. Just being cautious."

Everything happened too fast. This was not what I wished for. I FaceTimed Mom right away. "Please let me come in. I'm so scared," I begged.

"You can't. It's too dangerous." Mom's voice was strong.

"But kids can't get the virus!" I felt guilty for raising my voice when Mom and Dad were sick.

"Only some kids. I need to rest." She gave me a good night kiss over the phone.

Now that Dad was almost better, it was his turn to help Mom.

After a week in isolation, Mom's cough went deep into her lungs. Dad said her asthma made the symptoms worse.

Dad called an ambulance that would take Mom to the only hospital with a bed.

Mom looked pale and fragile on FaceTime. Her green eyes were outlined by red inflamed eyelids like a ring of fire surrounded them.

"Promise me…" The cough took her breath away and rattled in her lungs. "…you will always have hope."

"I promise." I'd say anything to make her feel better. "Mom?"

She did not answer. *She was going to die.* I collapsed, losing track of time and place.

Minutes passed, or maybe it was hours.

The ambulance pulled up without a sound. Three paramedics got out wearing white body suits, helmets, and oxygen tanks on their backs.

I grabbed my mask and ran up the stairs ahead of them and stood near Dad who was holding Mom's hand. I think I saw her smile when she saw me, but she couldn't speak. The flesh on her fingers was peeling off, exposing yellow tissue underneath. Her arms and legs had blisters and red sores that she tried to hide from me. I reached out to touch her, but her skin was so raw I thought it would hurt her. I pulled my hand back. Her hair fell in clumps around her shoulders like thick black ropes that I wanted to climb. Climb back in time when we were at the fountain before all this started. Or maybe even further, to a place *before* we existed when we were just particles in space.

Life went into slow motion, or maybe it stopped. The lady that wore neon yellow Nikes led me out of the room and took me downstairs. She sat with me.

A shorter lady in combat boots and a man in white tennis shoes carried Mom on the stretcher that had a tent on top with tubes and wires going in and out of it. Mom was in there somewhere. I watched them like a hawk tracking a rabbit.

The Nike lady was on the radio. She told the person on the other end, "She's in critical condition."

"Not my mother. It's a mistake," I said.

She glanced at me and finished up her call.

The ambulance disappeared into the yellow smoke. Dad was in the other room on the phone.

I sat on the edge of my bed and cried until there was nothing left inside me. What would I do without my mom? A hot, dry sadness blew through me. It parched my insides. I was hollow, a dead seed blowing in the wind. I wanted to be part of something like a grove of sequoia trees, a pack of wolves, flock of birds, or a pod of whales.

It was almost dark when Dad got a call from the hospital.

He came into my room and sat next to me on the bed. "She's on a ventilator and stabilizing."

"Will she be okay?" I asked.

"She's the strongest lady I know. If anyone can recover from this virus, she can."

"I hope so." I hugged my dad for the first time in years.

My phone chirped with a picture of Emmitt. I lifted it to my ear. That simple movement felt unfamiliar. I changed or the world changed.

"How are you?" Emmitt asked.

My feelings burst like solar flares. I was consumed by grief that I couldn't put to words. I managed to tell him that my mom was in ICU. The words did not feel like they were mine. It was not my mother. Someone else left our house in that ambulance.

Everything I knew and trusted was taken away from me. My mother, the mountains, the air. The predictability of my life was over. It was not supposed to happen like this. Not this fast. Not this soon. Not all at once. Yet here we were. In the middle of rapid climate change, droughts and fires, and a deadly virus. And the only thing I wanted was to be near Emmitt.

"Can you meet me at the fountain?" I asked.

"I'll be there in five minutes," he said.

I hung up, placed one of my letters to Emmitt in my backpack, and left.

Ash covered everything like Earth was cremated. I was on sacred ground and I tried not to disturb anything. It was quiet except for the woodpecker that tapped in the distance. The sound of its belonging. *What was my sound?*

The Azolla ferns spread out over the surface of Virginia Lake like a green carpet.

I wished my mother's lungs could breathe through the virus like the ferns did through the fires and smoke. If we were made from the same matter that formed life long ago, there was hope we would survive. Maybe not in the same form, or in ways we were accustomed to, but on some molecular level we would live. I was comforted knowing that we were part of something bigger than us.

The moon's gaze was steady. Silent. Observant.

Emmitt took my hands and held them between his. He brought them to his chest and kissed them. I cried. We stood there for a while holding each other.

"I brought something for you." I gave Emmitt one of my Indian head nickels. "Let's make a wish, or two."

We tossed our coins. The letter would come next.

Community Spread

Stephanie King

"Alexis, did you hear me?" Her mom entered the combined kitchen and family room from the hall, her heels clacking on the hardwood. "I need you to watch Dillon today. I have showings this afternoon."

"What?" Alexis plucked the bud from her ear, folded both legs on the sofa and scooched upright. She saw that her mother was dressed for work in a floral wrap dress and kitten-heel shoes. Her hair was long and thick with golden highlights that required hours in a salon chair and a decent amount of cash. These days it was serviced by her long-time hairdresser who was now sneaking in house calls for his most discreet clients.

"Wait," Alexis said. "You get to go out? I thought you weren't allowed to work. You know, 'safer at home' and all that."

"Lucky for me, I get to work. Real estate is an essential business."

Alexis slouched across the sectional sofa with one leg stretched along the cushions and one leg hanging to the floor. She turned back to her phone to see what she'd missed on

SnapChat. Probably more variations on the look-at-me-in-quarantine theme. She had nothing to post. She was so sick of quarantine.

"So, can you help me out?" her mother asked.

Alexis sensed an opportunity to negotiate.

"I need some new AirPods."

Her mom pulled her oversized Louis tote off one of the stools that surrounded the gigantic marble kitchen island and rifled for her wallet. She stood alongside the back of the sectional and raised an eyebrow. "And what's wrong with the ones you already have?" She gestured with the hand holding the credit card toward Alexis's ears where the tiny white buds peeked out from under her long, wavy hair.

Her green eyes tracked the gold AmEx card in her mother's hand.

"It's time to upgrade. I can give these to Dillon. Besides, don't you think I deserve something for being trapped at home?" Alexis twisted at the waist to face her mother and smiled.

Her mom bustled around the first floor opening windows. "Let's get some fresh air in here. It's going to be a beautiful day as soon as this fog lifts."

She turned the lock on the French doors to the poolside patio and used her foot to nudge a weighted ball wrapped in a nautical knot of rope to prop open the door. A salt-scented breeze wafted in. A tease given the governor had recently closed the beaches. Then she returned to the sofa where Alexis was sprawled and handed over her credit card.

Yes. Got it.

"Don't store it in ApplePay," her mother said.

"Yeah, sure, whatever."

She returned her focus to her phone screen, tapped in the credit card numbers and checked the box for expedited shipping. She turned to hand the credit card back to her mother and was startled to see her fastening a cloth mask across the bottom half of her face.

"For real?" Alexis said.

"Come on. We all need to do what we can to keep people from getting sick. Besides, this one matches my outfit," her mother said.

Alexis shrugged. "Won't it mess up your makeup?"

Her mother shook her head, gathered up her tote and swept out of the house. The front door clicked shut, and Alexis was stuck inside.

Just three weeks earlier she was loving her life as a college sophomore in Tucson. Now, because of some virus, a "pandemic" according to the social media feeds that kept popping up despite her attempts to block bad news, she was back under her mother's roof, cut off from her friends and saddled with her four-year-old brother. He was cute, and it wasn't his fault that their parents broke up shortly after he was born. Why they had another kid when it was clear Dad was getting action on the side was a mystery to Alexis. She wondered how Tinder was working out for her dad now.

Bored from watching YouTube projected onto the family room television, she turned her attention to her iPhone to see if anyone in her network had found something more interesting to do. Throughout the long days since the stay-at-home order went into effect, Alexis monitored her phone with the vigilance of an intelligence officer. She kept an eye on what her old friends from high school were up to as well as what her college friends, who were scattered across the country now that universities had shut down, were posting. From what Alexis could tell, no one was having fun. It was all so unfair.

Then, the doorbell rang, and Alexis bolted off the couch to the kitchen countertop where the screen to the door monitor rested. She watched as a delivery guy retreated to his van. *There's no way her AirPods could have arrived this fast.* Still, these days the arrival of a package counted as an event, and she bounded down the hall and pulled open the front door. She grabbed a large can of Lysol off a side table in the foyer and sprayed a shroud of disinfectant around the large cardboard box resting on her front porch. Her mother must have ordered something.

When the mist dissipated, she ripped off the packing tape and wrenched open the flaps not bothering to control her impulsiveness. *Toilet paper? What a fucking disappointment.* She bent to check the label. *Mrs. Harold Gerber. Oops.* The package wasn't even theirs.

She debated leaving it then thought about her neighbors. She thought back to when her dad left her mom. How it felt like the other women in their cul-de-sac were rooting against them in some messed up swirl of suburban marriage competition. Except Mrs. Gerber. How the old lady had brought over lasagna, figuring that her mom was too distracted by her problems to cook for her kids. It wasn't her fault she didn't know the only person in the house who still ate pasta was Dillon.

She put on a bandana and rubber gloves and carried the package to the neighboring house in the cul-de-sac.

Mrs. Gerber opened the front door looking ten years older than when she'd last seen her. Always whippet thin, her slimness had begun to morph from fashion to frailty. The mask covering her face didn't help. Come to think of it, had she seen Mrs. Gerber leave her house since all this started?

Alexis tipped the corners of her lips up in a tight smile behind the bandana but couldn't quite meet Mrs. Gerber's eyes. *Did she remember when she chased Alexis and her middle school friends down the street after they nabbed the whole bowl of Halloween candy from her porch?*

Her gaze flicked up to see if Mrs. Gerber still held this resentment as she toed the box on the porch.

"This came to our house, but it's for you."

"Thank you, Alexis." The old woman's eyes smiled over her mask.

"Sorry. I opened it. I thought it was for us," Alexis said. "But I disinfected it for you."

Mrs. Gerber chuckled. "That was kind. I can't be too careful. My heart condition puts me at risk with this virus." She leaned down and plucked a roll from the box and extended it to Alexis. "Here, take a roll for your family," she said. "It's in short supply you know."

"I'm good." Alexis swiveled toward her house then paused. She turned back to face her neighbor. "But thanks." She stooped to lift the large box off the porch. "Do you want me to set it inside for you?"

Back at home, Alexis heard a shout followed by a blast of music that sounded like it was coming from the backyard. She jogged up the stairs to the bedrooms where she would have a better view of the neighborhood. On the way, she peeked into her brother's room and found him lying on his stomach on the floor amid piles of toys and gadgets, face pressed into an iPad. Even though it was after noon he still wore his Aquaman pajamas. *Had he eaten yet today?*

She continued down the hallway to the master bedroom where the curtains ruffled in the breeze off the ocean just a quarter mile away. She scurried to the windows that overlooked the backyard and leaned out.

"Bruh. You got to chug it," a tall, broad-shouldered boy Alexis recognized from Harbor High School said. His family must have moved to the cul-de-sac that backed to hers while she was away at school. His sandy brown hair hadn't been trimmed in a while and the tips were bleached by the sun or chlorine. *Water polo*, she remembered. *Yum.*

In the yard visible over her back fence, a group of about fifteen boys gathered in the clear, bright sunshine that chased off the early morning coat of marine layer. They'd taken the initiative to set up two makeshift tables from sheets of plywood balanced on sawhorses, no doubt lifted from one of the many construction sites that dotted their neighborhood as homeowners strove to outdo each other. They bounced ping pong balls into red Solo cups, one table in competition with the other, while a bass line thrummed from the outdoor speakers.

Alexis plucked her phone from the waistband of her stretch pants and took a video of the backyard scene. She typed `quarantine party near my house` and sent the message and video clip to a group of girlfriends she knew from high school.

Text messages flew back and forth, alert tones pinging like a modern-day Morse code, as Alexis assembled a crew to crash the party.

Nikki texted to the group: `do i need to wear a mask`, and the group responded,
`boo`
`no, lame`
Alexis typed: `don't need to outside duh`

In her room, she pulled off the black Lululemon leggings she had been living in since the beginning of the shutdown and slid on a pair of terrycloth shorts and a strappy halter top. She twisted to check her backside in the mirror fastened to her closet door. *Yep, just the right amount of bum cleavage.* She pouted her lips and snapped a pic of herself reflected in the mirror. She would put together a story on Instagram to make her college friends from Arizona and Texas jealous.

She felt a shot of adrenaline every time her phone dinged with a message from a friend: so psyched, you rock alexis, saving us from lockdown boredom. It had been three weeks since she partied. She had suffered long enough.

In her bathroom she spritzed her tangled waves of blond hair with salt spray then finger-combed it for a tousled, just-back-from-the-beach look. She swiped mascara across her lashes and smeared lip gloss over her lips. Sniffing her armpits, she snatched a stick of deodorant from the basket next to her bathroom sink and rolled on two coats.

Rap music pulsed from next door, and the boys' laughter, shouting and cursing rose in volume, too. Alexis hoped her little brother wasn't hearing this. For all the time he spent on the internet, though, she figured there probably wasn't anything he hadn't already heard.

Shit…Dillon.

She was supposed to watch him. And, she couldn't wait until her mom got home from work. She might not let Alexis go to the party given the coronavirus thing. It's not like she knew anyone who was sick. And didn't the president say it was just like the flu? She was pissed that everyone had to suffer to save the old folks living in nursing homes. The way she saw it, they'd already lived their lives. Why not let her live hers?

She checked herself in the mirror one last time and smiled. *Nailed it.* She looked hot without looking like she tried too hard. Her phone buzzed with more incoming messages: you ready?, we r close.

Alexis padded over to her brother's room. He hadn't moved since she last peeked in. His white-blond curls—a gift wasted on a boy—fell over his screen-glazed eyes.

"Hey, bud." Alexis picked her route across her brother's carpet littered with loose Lego pieces. When he didn't look up from his tablet, she used her bare toe to prod under his armpit.

"Hey," her brother said, rolling side to side on his stomach to avoid her toe. A scowl erupted across his little face at the interruption.

Alexis softened. Even when irritated, her brother made her smile.

"Mom said you can't stay on your iPad all day. She wants me to put a movie on for you. Come to the family room." Alexis worked to keep her voice upbeat with the promise of fun.

Dillon ignored her. The incessant binging of her phone in her pocket acted on her nerves like an alarm clock without a snooze button. Her friends were going to show up any minute.

She bent down and plucked the iPad from her brother's hand, and he started to wail.

"Give that baaaaccckkkk." He squinched his eyes shut, and his face reddened.

"C'mon. I know where Mom hides the Nutella." Alexis tucked the iPad under her arm and spun out of the room. Her little brother scrambled up off the floor and trotted on bare feet behind her.

Five minutes later, her brother settled onto the sofa and watched his favorite superheroes cartoon with chocolate hazelnut cream smeared across his lips. Alexis found her flip-flops under a pair of water wings near the pool. She was ready to go.

She stepped into the family room, knocked aside the doorstopper and pulled the patio door shut behind her as her phone pinged– `we r outside`. "I'm just going to be at the house behind ours if you need anything," Alexis called to her brother as she walked through the house and out the front door.

The four girls plus Alexis, each dressed in candy-colored summer clothes that set off their Southern California tans, gathered in front of the boy's house. They pushed through a gate propped open on the side of the house and walked toward the music. The party had swelled in size to nearly thirty people. Alexis was disappointed to see other girls milling through the backyard, but the ratio was still in their favor. Lubricated with cheap beer and spiked seltzer, the boys welcomed the pretty new arrivals.

Alexis's friend, Vanessa, home from Tulane and a day-drinking pro, lifted the six-pack of hard seltzer to the water polo boy in a greeting salute before dumping the cans into a large ice cooler. Nikki swiped five Solo cups from the tower stack on the built-in barbeque and started shoveling in ice.

Alexis scanned the scene. The backyard was small and fenced in, the lawn crowded with fit and tanned bodies reveling in the opportunity to move among their kind after weeks of being cooped up. Over the back fence sat Alexis's backyard and, to the right of it, Mrs. Gerber's house.

Movement from the second floor of her neighbor's house caught her eye. Mrs. Gerber came out on her balcony and shouted something at the teens, but her voice was drowned out by the music. She wore a mask as if the air from the party might waft to her house and infect her. She shook her head at the kids clustering on the lawn then scurried back into her house through the glass doors. Alexis tensed with annoyance and hoped the woman wouldn't tell her mom she saw her over here.

Alexis sidled between the two plywood tables to watch the beer pong tournament. At U of A she was the champion of her freshman year dorm. She had to give up carbs and switch to hard liquor, though, after gaining the freshman fifteen. Out of practice now, she doubted she'd be able to hold her own in this crowd and held her red cup aloft to Nikki who added an extra shot of tequila to her drink.

Filled with liquid courage, Alexis found the boy she had seen from her mother's bedroom window moving through the crowd in red swim trunks. Up close, she admired his defined shoulders and chest. She caught a glimpse of his caramel eyes. She remembered his name.

"Casey, hi," she said as she pounced, swatting his muscular bicep. "Hey, it's so great you're having this party. I've been so bored."

"Yeah, right. I can't believe they closed down colleges," he said.

"I know, right?" Alexis said.

Then Casey said, "My parents are so pissed. USC is like one of the most expensive schools. All that money for me to sit in their house and watch my classes on a laptop."

Alexis couldn't believe her luck. Maybe things were looking up after all with this hot guy in her neighborhood this summer. She forced her brain, just beginning to feel muddied by the liquor, to focus on something to say to keep this boy's focus on her when suddenly sirens cut through the music, and Casey looked around.

Alexis followed his eyes surveying the yard and surrounding homes. Her gaze halted, like Casey's, on Mrs. Gerber's house. Her window was empty.

"Fuck," he said as he gestured at her house. "That old bat probably called the cops on us."

Alexis bristled. *That was kinda harsh. No lasagna for him.*

"She's probably just freaked out about the crowd. Community spread and all that," Alexis said. She wracked her brain to think of something to say that would get her conversation with Casey back on track.

He ignored her and signaled to a guy with his baseball cap on overdrive standing next to the speakers to shut the music off.

She giggled and looked through her lashes trying to recapture Casey's attention.

But he seemed distracted. *Would the police really shut down a backyard party? Could they?* That was the problem, she guessed, with living in such a low-crime town. They had nothing better to do.

He pumped his arms to quiet the crowd as the sirens grew closer, and Alexis noticed a tattoo on the inside of his bicep. She'd make it her mission this summer to get a closer look at that.

The sirens, growing closer only seconds before, had begun to fade. *They must be headed to another cul-de-sac,* Alexis thought. She saw Casey approach the music table no doubt to get the party started again and considered how to regain his attention when she heard a commotion from the other side of the fence. From her yard. *What the hell?*

The music erupted and the partygoers cheered. She debated whether to follow Casey or re-join her girlfriends when an uncomfortable thought popped into her brain.

Shit… Dillon.

Alexis dropped her cup and spun away from the partiers. Her flip-flops fell off as she sprinted toward the back of the yard. The sound of the siren returned—*were they now in her cul-de-sac?*—and reached a crescendo as she stood at the fence.

She took three long strides to an olive tree planted in the corner alongside the fence and scrambled up on its low branches. Six feet up she flung her arms over the top and hoisted herself the last few inches to peer to the other side.

Her brain, reverberating with rap music and struggling under the weight of the shot of tequila, tried to make sense of the scene unfolding over the fence.

Mrs. Gerber entered the backyard from the side clad in a housedress and slippers, mask affixed to her face. She winced against the stark bright sun making Alexis think it had been awhile since she had been outside. The old woman stepped quickly but ran her hand for balance along the stone wall that separated their yards. Her other hand rested on her chest.

What the hell was she doing?

Moments later, two paramedics entered trailing Mrs. Gerber.

Alexis's eyes darted to the pool as the paramedics sprinted to its side. There, her brother, still in his Aquaman pajamas, lay floating face down in the water. His curls encircled his head like a halo. His inflated water wings kept his body at the surface.

Alexis gripped the fence and flung her legs over the top, dropping down to her yard. She choked back the bile that rose in her throat as shame invaded her belly like poison. *How could she have left him alone?* She knew better. She'd even taken babysitter training in high school—first aid and everything.

Through tears pooling in her eyes, she watched stunned as her little brother flipped onto his back. A big grin spread across his small face as he stared up at his unexpected audience. "I can hold my breath for a long time," he said, shouting over the music.

Alexis exhaled not realizing she had been holding her breath. Still planted where she landed, her body sagged against the fence as adrenaline drained from her system. Her brother splashed and paddled in the pool. *God, that was a close call.*

"That's great, buddy," Alexis said as she collected herself. She pushed herself off the fence and walked toward the pool, her limbs loose with relief. "But you scared us. Next time you need to come get me. You know you can't be in the pool by yourself."

She took a few hesitant steps toward the paramedics. She wanted to thank them and Mrs. Gerber, too. She noticed the old woman hung back from the paramedics close to the side wall.

"Listen, you ought to have a security fence around this pool. Especially with a little one living here," one of the paramedics said. He was short and stocky with close-cropped black hair. Alexis straightened her posture, a shield to his scolding.

"You're right," Alexis nodded. The shock of the emergency made her feel clearheaded. "Thank you for coming. I'll tell my mother." She guided the paramedics past Mrs. Gerber and through the side yard anxious to get them out before her mom came home.

Her neighbor remained resting against the wall that separated their yards. Alexis presumed she had called 9-1-1. She felt responsible for scaring her and wanted to thank her for once again showing kindness to her family.

Before she could do that, her mother, returning home from work to an ambulance parked in front of her house, rushed through the family room and onto the patio.

Busted. Alexis's mind scrambled with thoughts on how to explain this to her mother. She wished she had time to agree to a story with her brother, but it was too late now.

No, she'd come clean. She'd learned her lesson. No party was worth those seconds of sickening fear when she thought her little brother had drowned. Thank God their neighbor was looking out for them.

But her mother did nothing more than cast a worried glance her way before sprinting across the patio toward Mrs. Gerber, stumbling as her heels sunk into the lawn where the patio ended.

Chills crawled across Alexis's skin, and her stomach lurched and twisted. There, on the ground at the base of the wall, lay Mrs. Gerber. Collapsed.

Her mother yelled, "Help!" and dropped to her knees, fumbling for her phone.

Alexis raced to her side and dove to the ground. She yanked the mask from the old woman's face to check for breathing. Feeling none, she started CPR compressions as her arms trembled and tears streaked down her cheeks.

Mary and Joseph

Jan Mannino

Small, healed lacerations on his fingers, dirt tattooed on calloused skin, grease wedged under short stubby fingernails, all indications he was a working man. Mechanic? Carpenter? Gardner? Construction worker? It didn't matter.

She adjusted the pulse oximeter finger probe, checked the IV site, making sure it worked well enough to handle the drugs she was about to administer. She stopped for a second to notice the amateurish tattoo on his forearm, *Joey 10/5/2018*.

The ICU nurses and respiratory therapists shifted impatiently from foot to foot. "Come on, just intubate him. We have other sick patients."

In her double mask, a clear shield over an N95, protective googles, yellow disposable gown, and paper shower cap style hair covering, Mary leaned over the young man and waved her hands at the others to wait.

"My name is Mary. I am your nurse-anesthesiologist and will be giving some medication to relax you, so I can put a breathing tube down your windpipe. We will then connect it to a ventilator that will breathe for you and let your lungs heal while we treat the coronavirus."

His pupils dilated in fear, and his mouth opened as he struggled to get in enough oxygen through the clear, green plastic mask covering his mouth and nose. Yet he nodded to show he understood and agreed.

One of the nurses asked if she could now give the sedation. Mary answered, "No, I like to give the drugs myself."

She slowly titrated in the midazolam to relax him and watched as his eyelids closed but continued to flutter. "I see your name is Joseph. Is Joey your son?" she whispered in his ear. He nodded as his lips parted in a smile. "We will take good care of you, so you can take good care of Joey when you are better."

A tear trickled down his cheek as he drifted off to a sedated sleep.

After the muscle relaxant took effect, Mary skillfully inserted the cold, surgical steel laryngoscope in his mouth, identified the vocal cords, and inserted the endotracheal tube. End-tidal carbon dioxide readings showed the tube was properly placed. The numbers on the pulse oximeter moved rapidly from the hypoxic 70 to a perfect 98. Mary used a stethoscope to assure both lungs were being ventilated. She closed her eyes to concentrate on the cracking and wheezing, signs of lung damage from the small, deadly virus. There was a satisfied sigh from the nurses and therapists at the bedside as they took over to secure the tube and attach the ventilator. A successful intubation was the first step in letting the ventilator take over his breathing.

She squeezed his hand again as she moved away and felt his return acknowledgement.

Her shift over, Mary sat on a wooden bench in the locker room while changing into her street clothes. She heard beeping monitors, an occasional alarm, the swishing sounds of ventilators breathing for patients, and the quiet hustle of the staff who were dedicated to caring for the sick and dying.

A gush of tears cascaded down her cheeks as she put her head down and covered her face with both hands. Someone sat next to her and offered a bottle of chilled water.

"Are you ok?"

"No, I am not ok." She tossed her scrubs in the contaminated laundry basket, pulled on jeans and sweatshirt, and clocked out of the twelve-hour shift. "I'll be back tomorrow."

Womb

Rosalia Mattern

Even now, more than a year after the fires, she still woke to the stench of smoke. This incinerated shell was their forever home, an expression that felt trite compared to the other phrases. Forever Home. Worldwide Pandemic. Disastrous Diplomacy. Hijacked Internet. Global War. Humankind destroyed itself in clichés.

She stepped over the sleeping bodies of her mother, brown and wrinkled, face up, arms spread, snoring like royalty, and her daughter, wound in a tight fetal in the corner, long hair plastered with perspiration. The child seemed to have grown another foot since her tenth birthday the week before.

A canopy of burnt roofs and charred walls, theirs and those pilfered from the wrecked homes surrounding them, camouflaged the courtyard and remains of their house, hiding them from pillagers and contamination. They lived in hidden darkness, within a corpse puzzled from gutted houses. Light sacrificed to safety. Only survival mattered.

The woman remembered how the fires first raged a couple of years after the pandemic began, after the collapse of international governments. News reports described paranoid leaders who sabotaged research. When video footage emerged of virus super strains being unleashed into rival populations, she and her neighbors gathered at the edges of their driveways in disbelief. Many wept at the inhumanity. If they had known the brutality to come, they would have saved their tears.

A series of routines filled her days now, a desperate grasp at normalcy. Morning watch included an inspection of all entrances. The front gate lay hidden from the street and overhead patrols, camouflaged by overgrown hedges and deliberately placed debris. Their home, safely tucked within the darkness of its charred shell. Twice daily the woman shook the locks and examined the latches. Check. Recheck. Routine was her sanity.

Yet, the panicked screams of her neighbors still filled her ears as she relived the scorching heat of an inferno on their suburban cul-de-sac. The absence of leadership gave rise to militarized survivors who feared nothing after surviving the virus. The Immune, as they called themselves, plundered, vandalized, and much worse. What they couldn't carry away, they burned to the ground. What didn't burn was shot.

Her family could not outrun the attacks, and even if they could, where would they go? Instead, they hid behind the walls of their stuccoed patio and covered themselves with blankets and towels drenched in water. They huddled and prayed for hours, maybe days, until all sounds ceased. She remembered staggering to the street, her husband's arm around her shoulder; the rest of the family followed in a dazed single file line. The devastation left them in silent shock. Theirs the only house that still stood. Their forever home fulfilled its promise.

Relief turned to trepidation as the realization set in. Like a neon sign among its fire-ravaged neighbors, the house telegraphed their survival to the Immune.

You failed. They're still alive.

The Immune would return and punish them for the audacity to endure. She remembered her husband, father and brother frantically grabbing anything that could burn: an old welding torch, BBQ tanks, gas tanks and even the matches. Her mother turned on all the faucets in the house and gathered hoses from their yard and their neighbors' and filled every container with water. She and her daughter moved pillows, blankets, clothes, and whatever else seemed crucial for survival, into the yard away from the flames, a hasty triage of material possessions. They scorched the Sherwin-Williams sunset beige walls. The slate roof was sacrificed deliberately, but most of the second floor was lost unintentionally when the flames flared out of control. They set fire to their forever home, not all of it. Just enough to make it look like the other houses. Just enough to be left alone. That year everything burned. Everything but the virus.

As she made her morning rounds, she glimpsed the Ruger revolver atop knives and hammers in the makeshift collection of weapons piled in the basket that once held the garden hose. Her husband warned her.

Never touch the gun unless you are prepared to kill.

She assumed she could do whatever survival required but wondered if killing would place her on the same moral plane as those she loathed: corrupt leaders and the heartless Immune.

Her foot stepped onto the worn wooden crate. In the first year, it brought their produce. Now the crate proved invaluable for its functionality. Chair, container, backrest, and on this early morning, stepstool. Adapt or die. Life flourished within their dark, concealed world because they adapted. The drained spa, with its custom Catalina tile, housed a sufficient garden from her husband's foresight to harvest seeds from every fruit and vegetable they'd eaten. Water continuously distilled from muddy puddles using top-of-the-line REI camping equipment and custom homebrew kits. Dry goods and pharmaceuticals stockpiled from looted drugstores and pharmacies. They could survive here forever if they had to. If they wanted to. Survival, adaptation, death? Which one was the worst fate? Darkness made it hard to distinguish.

She strained for a glimpse of what laid beyond their gloomy walls. Dirty, stringy hair caught on the branches of the bougainvillea as she craned her neck through a concealed break in the hedge. Ash-black and charred like every surface that sheltered them, the plant long ago gave up on its fuchsia blossoms. Some leaves still stubbornly grew in the gray wasteland, refused to surrender. She ran her fingers over a stem of green. An unspoken promise of solidarity.

We'll keep living if you will.

The last of their neighbors left months before, unable to endure the stamina required of survival, thinking that surrender to whomever held power now was easier than hiding. Yet every day the woman hoped. Hoped the whispered rumors she heard in the early years, of vaccines and cures distributed by the underground, were true. Hoped that people she loved still survived somewhere beyond their tract. Hoped, that on this day, the sun might burst through Earth's littered atmosphere and warm her face. She opened her eyelids in a soundless *Amen,* squinting in the daylight because of her weakened retinas. The charcoal dust stung her eyes. A blanket of gray film covered the block, like a perverse winter scene. God's cruel answer. She spat the gravelly saliva from her mouth, a blasphemous act of defiance.

Her mother threw wrinkled fists in the air for one final stretch and rose from the concrete floor to offer a hug. The woman opened her arms in reply. During the first forty days, her mother laid immobile on one of the twin beds: legs, arms and mouth imprisoned by a degenerative neurological condition. A best friend from high school questioned taking the mother from a nursing home into their household.

She's eighty-eight. Is it even worth it?

Her mother rejuvenated with every month in their cocoon. When the feeding tube formula ran out, her mother fed herself from the pantry. After the last Depends was worn, she walked to the toilet. Like Lazarus commanded to rise from the tomb, her mother escaped the bony grip of death. Adapt or die. The high school friend succumbed to the virus early on, yet her mother thrived in this blackened existence.

The woman bent down to wipe dust from her daughter's face. A Sisyphean task. Since the year of the great fires, soot permanently hung in the air. The virus had never entered their courtyard. The woman wouldn't allow it. She was methodical with sterilization, bleaching every surface daily, like the doctors in hospitals or the scientists in labs. Routine was her sanity.

Her mother lit the gas camping stove and put on a small aluminum pot. She gathered the ingredients for Filipino rice porridge: a cup of rice, a brown onion and ginger.

Lugau, will be good today.

The voice was strong and clear. Her mother moved nimbly. Any trace of her pre-pandemic paralysis evaporated. She prepared the meal for the three of them. They were only three now.

Thinking about the early years disturbed the woman. It allowed mistakes and doubt to haunt her. They wore masks. Of course, they wore masks. They quarantined. Then they all donned the mandatory hazmat suits. They submitted to the humiliating disinfecting sprays, running through human car washes. Who could have imagined the marathon of monotony survival brought? Why did they hoard useless money instead of fuel? Why had they prepared for loss of utilities like water and electricity, but not Wi-Fi and cell service? Why didn't the men stay?

She wanted to sympathize with the men. Now blame, anger, and resentment sat at the family table in the seats they once occupied. Shortly after the Great Fires began, her husband, a retired firefighter, begged her to understand. How could he stay here, safe in their hideout, while fires raged? How could he live with himself? Her brother left a month after. He was in love before the quarantine. He needed to find his girl and be with her. The last to leave was the woman's father. He played Don Quixote screaming day and night as he battled the invisible windmills of the virus. She tied his arms to a post in the patio where he slept, to keep him home, hidden and safe. He stole away anyway, in the darkest part of the night, leaving behind bloodied ropes, and taking with him a brain riddled with Alzheimer's. A year without the men and the women still survived.

In the courtyard, her mother placed a firm hand on the woman's shoulder and spoke in Tagalog.

Tumigil sa pag-alala. Stop remembering.

She stared into her mother's black, lucid eyes and covered the hand with her own. A familiarity radiated from the contact, gestures and intonations the woman hadn't experienced in decades. There was a great deal now about her mother that was foreign to her. She'd lived so long with a mother who was dying that she could barely recognize this mother who was filled with life.

After breakfast, while her mother tidied the pans and her daughter hopscotched in the courtyard, the woman heard the voice and froze in horror.

Let me in. I know you are there. I finally found you. I smell the lugua. Please help me.

She inhaled deeply but still couldn't get enough air. Her mind raced, running through all the possible outcomes tied to this voice. She collapsed onto the crate, put her hands on her knees and focused on the lock ten feet away. She needed to think. Their caution bordered on obsession. No one could have known they were living in the dark shell of the burned-out house. She looked skyward in a desperate plea but only the charred patio covering met her eyes. The voice pressed on.

Please I'm sick. I can't live out here anymore.

His weeping, unhuman, like a wounded dog. The three remained silent in the darkness and listened to his cries. They all recognized his voice. Her mother made the sign of the cross and clasped both hands in prayer. Her daughter scooted on the crate next to her and shook her arm. The woman held up a hand to stop the pleading. Methodically, she considered the situation. Was he followed? Was he armed? Was he infected?

She motioned silently for her daughter to stay on the crate in the safety of the courtyard's darkness. Even before she saw his face, the woman knew it would be her father she'd spy through the hedge. He was thinner since the last time she saw him, hair longer, but his eyes were still wildly unfocused. Where was he this past year? How did he find his way here?

His mask was purple.

She drew her head back. Panic grabbed her pulsating heart and squeezed it. Before they lost the internet, friends from the CDC shared the government's highly classified rainbow categorizations. Triage centers distributed light-colored masks like yellow and orange to patients with original virus infections, the less malignant first- and second-year strains. As the virus spread, it grew more virulent, deadly, and untreatable. The government refused to reveal the color coding to the public.

Never go near anyone with a purple or black mask.

That was the last email received. She had to get him away from their gate. She had to get him to leave them alone. Only survival mattered.

The Ruger. She wouldn't use it. How could she shoot her own father? But she could brandish it and make him leave. Even a man with Alzheimer's would understand that. As she returned from the hedge, the woman retrieved the gun from the basket of weapons and contemplated the weight and mechanics of the firearm. She glanced at the crate where she told her daughter to remain. It was empty. Her father's voice continued.

Apo. Granddaughter. Thank you. Thank you. Please hurry. I'm sick. Let me in.

The child skipped to the gate and whispered to him as she moved the numbers on the combination lock. He spoke quickly. Urgently. The woman witnessed her father's manipulation and her daughter's willingness to please.

The scene moved in slow motion. Even now as she recalled it, each action seemed to last an hour. She yelled out to them both.

Stop.

The moment he heard the click of the tumblers, her father pushed the gate open with great force. In that instant, the effects of the virus were obvious: the bloodshot eyes, the purple fingers, and the blotchy skin.

Without thinking, she squeezed the trigger. The hammer on the single-action gun dropped instantly. Her daughter fell back from the momentum of the swinging gate and then reflexively reached forward to prevent her fall, toward her grandfather, toward the flash of purple. Her hand reached him the same instant the bullet, which struck his cheek, exploded.

The blood spatter was immediate and widespread. Even in the darkness, the woman could see surfaces in the courtyard glisten red. She watched as her daughter rubbed first nose, then eyes, and finally mouth with the back of her small, bloodied hands.

The woman gripped the Ruger, poised to shoot her father again if necessary. It wasn't necessary. Her aim was precise and lethal. She knew now that she could kill. If she could relive the moment, she would have shot him sooner, when she first saw him on the other side of the fence. If she could relive it again, she would have waited at the gate and shot him as he turned the corner onto the cul-de-sac. The murder became increasingly premeditated with each replay. She moved to apologize to her mother, but the woman felt no remorse. Neither did her mother ask for contrition. They both understood the price of survival.

In the days that followed, the virus moved through the child ravenously. The woman wept bitterly as she wiped her daughter's face. They disinfected themselves as well as they could, surprised the instinct to survive was so ingrained. During the night, the woman and her mother pulled on their government recommended hazmat suits, gathered all the pieces of her father and buried him in a yard four houses away. In the darkness, they worked clinically, systematically for the remainder of the night and bleached every surface blood had touched.

She isn't infected. She isn't infected.

Could willing it make it so? Her daughter's forehead burned with fever. She grabbed a fresh, cool cloth from the bucket, squeezed the water from it, and placed it across her daughter's forehead. No movement. Only a weak moan. The woman recalled the first months of quarantine, her daughter's silly songs, funny riddles and zestful spirit, willed them all to endure the miserable confinement. In the years since, the mere presence of her youth, innocence, and vitality gave them reason to persevere. How would she endure anymore without her child?

She inventoried the common symptoms in her daughter: spiked fever, loss of energy, taste and appetite. Then the elevated symptoms appeared: loss of consciousness, purple extremities and blood trickling from the corners of her mouth. She couldn't see in the darkness, but she could smell the metallic odor of fresh blood.

They carried the child to the brightest part of the patio, by the garden in the back. The woman knelt on the ground and placed her daughter's head in her lap. She grabbed her mother's hand, placed it on her daughter's small chest and held it there and waited. Perhaps the same life force that retrieved her mother from the sick and dying, could do the same for her daughter.

Nothing.

She cradled her daughter's face and traced the skin she had memorized since the day of the child's birth. Her baby. Her only born. The woman covered her child with a blanket of loving whispers, determined she would leave this earth bathed in blessings and lullabies. Several minutes elapsed before she realized her daughter no longer breathed.

For the first time in the years since the quarantine began, the woman had no routine. She clicked through the lists in her mind, but they no longer made sense, as if the words reformed in a different language.

Again, she felt her mother's hand on her shoulder. She raised her head to a pink canopy of petunias. In her grief, the woman hadn't heard her mother rummaging through the scorched piles in the courtyard to find the child's favorite blanket, the one with pink flowers.

This would be her pall. The woman spread the blanket on the ground, and then placed her child in the center. She folded the edges of the pink fabric over tiny feet, hips, hands and face. Her daughter's long, dark hair cascaded from the top of the pink pall. She reached for the hair and caressed it between her fingers for a full minute before placing it within the tightly wrapped sheet.

She chose a smaller shovel, and not the same one she used days before to bury her father. In solemn rhythm, she placed her foot on the top of the shovel and rocked back and forth to loosen the earth. This precious life which came to life from darkness of her womb would now leave the world in another darkened womb, in this soft tissue of earth. The woman refused to wash her hands or change her clothes. She wore her daughter's new home beneath her fingernails and in her clothes and hair. The last thing she wanted to do was wash it off.

Weeks later, her grief felt even thicker. She sat on the crate in darkness, the last place her daughter sat, and stared at the gate.

If I could see it happen a differently, maybe it would happen that way. And then she could come back to me.

Her mother witnessed in solemn silence. She cooked the meals and washed the clothes. And because there was no one else to do it, her mother checked the gates and locks. The woman remained on the crate. No routine. No lists. No hope.

Her mother took her by the hand and walked her to the gate, unlocked it and pulled it open. She pushed the woman forward through the threshold and stood shoulder to shoulder with her in the light of the midday sun.

She will not come back to you. This isn't her life anymore. Is it yours? Hanapin ang iyong tahanan. Find your life.

The street was silent, as if everything, the birds and the wind itself, waited for her response.

I can't leave you alone. I need to take care of you.

A smile appeared on her mother's lips.

Can't you see? I've been taking care of you.

She looked to the sky, but the woman no longer hoped.

Who am I if I'm not taking care of somebody? What would I live for then?

Her mother reached for her hand and held it tightly.

Ang magtanong ay mabuhay. To ask those questions is the beginning of living. Go and ask your questions.

She kissed her mother on both cheeks and walked to the end of the cul-de-sac. She stood in the center of the street. Untethered. For the first time, responsible for only herself. Behind her stood the disguised cocoon. The home had protected them, but now her mother was sending her from that womb into the world. A second birth. If she wanted it.

Darkness had been the woman's nemesis. She loathed it, yet it had kept them all alive for a long time. Longer than most. Perhaps long enough. Unaccustomed to the sun, she raised her hand above her brow to shade her eyes and squinted to see what lay before her. In this second life, light would no longer be sacrificed. And survival mattered very little anymore.

New Talents
Marla Noel

Dead IV monitors stood on either side of the bed. I focused my eyes on the surroundings. This wasn't my bed or my house. A cord wrapped around bars on the left side of the bed had a red button at the end. I pushed the button and waited. Nothing happened. I sat up and grabbed the bars to make the room stop spinning. My fingernails, long, with remnants of nail polish scraped against my scalp as I brushed back tangled strands of hair from my face. A window stretching across one wall revealed darkness. A door to a dimly lit hallway stood open. I narrowed my eyes. I couldn't see a soul.

Two more beds on the other wall with curtains partially drawn revealed occupants. A hand draped over the bars of one bed and a foot protruded from bedsheets in the other. I stood and made sure my legs were stable before moving away from the bars. As I set both feet on the cold linoleum, a strength pulsed through me. Odd. A mirror, next to the bed, revealed a stranger. My face had thinned. My curly brown hair was long. Last I remembered, it was short, with a pricey haircut and highlights. Now, there was a thick line of grey, a punctuation over tangled strands of brown. I needed makeup. I looked old and haggard for my forty-five years. A white band hung loosely around my wrist. I closed my eyes to stave off confusion and fear. I must be in a hospital, but why?

I took in a deep breath and a putrid odor slammed my senses, like meat gone bad. I knew the smell. I'd practiced medicine before I agreed to bow out of the workforce years ago to be a mother. The odor of death emanated from the other beds. I tip-toed to the closest bed and grabbed onto a chair as I gazed at the horror. The mouth was open, eyes stared into space and white hair splayed across a pillow. Something yellow oozed to the floor. I choked down a gag, then moved to the other bed. I figured the person had been dead longer. Blonde hair framed a ghoulish face. The skin pulled away from the open mouth and eyes. A waxy green on its way to black circled the ears. My knees buckled. The chair next to the bed cushioned my fall.

My heart flipped a few times. My brain tried to make sense of what I saw. I staggered into the hall, my ass exposed to the cool air from the open hospital gown. I went from room to room and found similar scenes, rotting dead people. No one was at the nurse's station or in any of the halls. Computer screens were blank and when I picked up a phone to see if I could call, there was no sound, no dial tone. The phones were dead, like everything else around me.

I went back to my room and found my clothes in a bag next to the bed. As I pulled on my now baggy pants, I thought about the last thing I remembered. We were celebrating Larry's 50th birthday. I busied myself in the kitchen, putting finishing touches on the dinner. My husband and my in-laws, whom I referred to as outlaws, were on the back porch of our suburban Southern California home. Larry's sister, Sharon, sat on one side, and his mother, Betty, on the other. Larry looked content, holding onto his third vodka tonic, his thick grey hair around a tan face, blue eyes brighter than usual. His long athletic legs were extended and crossed at the ankles. Sharon's arms gyrated along with her animated conversation. I muttered to myself about the lack of help with dinner, but Larry did more than his fair share of supporting me and making all the household decisions, something I wasn't good at. The pool, on the other side of the patio, called to me. I'd missed my morning swim, too busy with company prep to get in my cherished exercise. I pulled one of the side dishes out of the refrigerator when a strange feeling flooded me, like I was immersed in a vat of boiling water. I sat at the kitchen table, letting the feeling pass. Nausea hit me like a speeding corvette, and I covered my mouth to stop the bile. Next thing I knew, I was on the floor looking up into Larry's face. I saw a strange look in his eyes before I blacked out.

I pulled on my blouse and was grateful for the sweater I found in the top drawer of the bed stand. I shivered, not sure if it was from the cool air in the halls or shock. My cell sat on the stand, still plugged in. I was never more grateful to see a cell phone in my life. My hands shook as I unplugged the phone, punched in my password, and called Larry's cell. No answer. At least the phone worked. I tried Betty's cell next. Again, no answer. My fifteen-year-old, Brittany, was almost responsible. She frequently skipped school and suffered from the self-centered demeanor of many teens, but she was basically a good kid. I punched in her code. My heart fluttered with joy when I heard her voice.

"Mom, is that you?" She started to cry a deep and desperate wail.

"Honey, yes it's me. What's wrong? Where's your dad?" I wanted to reach through the phone and hug her. I struggled to hear. My phone wasn't working right.

"I don't know. I don't know where anyone is." She managed to spill the words through gut-wrenching sobs. "Dad and me, we were okay for a while. He visited you every day. I wasn't allowed. Then he went to see you a couple of weeks ago and never came home. I've called him so many times."

"Are you all alone? Have you tried your grandma or grandpa?" I looked around for my purse. I had to get to her. If I could fly, I would have grown wings. "Are you okay?"

"Mom. I've tried them. I'm scared." Her sobs slowed. "I miss Dad. I don't know what to do. Please come home."

"Oh, my God." I took in a deep breath, confused. "I'll get there as soon as I can." My heart fractured, thinking about my baby, all alone.

With the phone cradled between my ear and shoulder, I found my purse in another drawer. There were a few twenties in my wallet. I could take a taxi home. I could hardly wait to get out of the room and away from the smell of death. My heart went out to my girl, tall, thin, and blonde, like her father. She had his blue eyes and great sense of humor. Unfortunately for her, she had my sense of style.

"Okay, Mom. Please hurry. I'm so scared," Brittany said. "I can't get anything on my phone, no news, no music. I can't reach any of my friends."

"I'm on my way," I said and hung up the phone.

I felt desperate to get to her, hold her in my arms and let her know she was safe, even if she wasn't.

I headed out into the hall and found the stairs. I didn't want to risk getting into an elevator. I felt light as a feather as I ran down the steps. So much energy. At the bottom, I shoved open the door to the hall and bumped into a stocky middle-aged gentleman.

"Holy Moses," he said as he ran his hands through his grey hair, which was slicked back into a ponytail. He wore jeans, tennis shoes, and a golf shirt.

"Sorry," I said. "I didn't mean to startle you." I backed up, not sure if I was happy or frightened to see another person.

"My lands." His smile looked as though it would crack his face. "I'm so happy to see someone else in this god-forsaken place besides the patients and those poor nurses on the third floor." His voice sounded like it was far away. It was as though my ears had cotton in them. I looked past the man. There was no one in the lobby or the halls. I wondered where everyone was.

"Me too," I said. I immediately liked his face with brown eyes, laugh lines, and a fast smile. "Where am I?"

"You're in the hospital," he said. "Saint Cecilia's." He put his hands in his pockets. "Name's Harley, like the motorcycle."

I strained to hear what he was saying. He took a step toward me.

"My name's Shelly." I said. I took a step back, not sure if I should trust this stranger.

"I need to get home, get to my daughter," I said. "Is there a taxi?"

Harley let out a laugh. "Lady, there are no taxis and no cars on the road. Most are too scared to go out. Those that are left anyway." He must have noticed the distressed look on my face. "I got a car out there." He nodded to the front lobby. "I can take you."

"I don't want to put you out," I said. I shifted uncomfortably. I wasn't about to get into a car with a stranger.

"I came to visit my mother on the third floor," he said. "She didn't make it. I've been trying to figure out how to get her buried." His eyes watered and he looked down. "Don't think it is possible with all of this stuff." He waved his hand at the uninhabited hallway.

"I'm so sorry," I said, not used to consoling a grieving person. I searched for the proper thing to say. Fortunately, he spoke before I stuck my foot in my mouth.

"She's out of her suffering," he said. "She hasn't been feeling well all year. Bum heart. This virus thing took care of her real quick."

"What virus?" I asked. I had to focus on his mouth to make sure I understood what he was saying.

"How long you been here?" His eyes caught on the band around my wrist, identifying me as a patient.

"I don't really know," I said. "I couldn't seem to find anyone alive on the floor I was on."

"Oh no," he said. "You musta been on the fourth floor. I heard they thought everyone up there was gone."

"They gave me up for dead?" I said, growing angry, then shrugged it off, not sure of my next steps.

"So many didn't make it. There are some of the staff on the second and third floor. A lot of them in the same boat as the patients," he said. He shook his head. "Not many left to take care of people. They must have thought you were too far gone. I had this myself a few months ago but got through it."

"I don't know how long I've been here. What day is it?" I asked.

"It's the thirtieth." He dug in his pocket and pulled out a key fob.

I thought back to Larry's birthday, the last day I remembered. It was the tenth of July. "I've been here most of July," I said.

He looked stunned for a moment. "Shelly, you said your name was Shelly, right?" I nodded. "It's the thirtieth of

October. Since you've been lounging around on the fourth floor," he said. "More than half the population of California has succumbed to this COVID 26."

I shook my head and tried to grasp what he was telling me. My heart skipped a beat. I wanted my husband. He would take care of everything. Was he still alive? My brain grappled with what Harley told me before I got the next surprise.

He looked at me and said. "You may be able to hear me." His lips were not moving. It was as though he shoved the words into my brain.

I jumped. He gave out a feeble chuckle. "There is something good from every crappy situation," he said. "Those who've had this, can't hear as well, but can communicate telepathically."

Oh my, I thought. He must have heard me. He smiled.

"Exactly, oh my." His words entered my head, before he started dancing around the lobby. He must be crazy. Maybe that's another side-effect. "For some silly-ass reason, for us survivors, our muscles and bones are stronger. I feel like I'm twenty all over again."

I backed up more and vowed I would definitely not get into a car with this man.

"I can see you don't believe me," he said after he stopped dancing. "Give it a try, go run down that hall, and see if you're winded at all."

"That's okay," I said. I needed to get away from this nut case. "I need to get home." I bowed away from the man and aimed for the front door. As I walked, I felt the strength and energy in my arms and legs. Maybe he wasn't a nut case.

Out front, there were no taxies or cars. I tried Uber and taxi services on my cell, then tried to call my car. The auto pickup on my Tesla would have worked if we were only a few miles closer. The air was crisp and surprisingly fresh, country fresh, unlike the smell of death I left behind. I started to pace as I thought through my predicament. I could walk home. We lived about eight hilly miles from the hospital, but it was doable. After a few minutes, Harley wandered out and stood next to me.

"Sorry for the dancing. You must think I'm crazy," he said. "It's just so nice to have this energy." He looked sheepish.

"It's okay," I said, although I didn't mean it.

"Where do you live?" This time he spoke the words. I tried to figure out which communication was better. The mind thing was easier.

"Laguna Niguel," I looked at Harley to see if he heard my thought. "Not far."

"I live in that direction," he said and nodded his head toward the parking lot and took off at a fast pace. "Let's go."

His movements were quick. I wasn't sure of his age, but pegged him to be around 50, close to Larry's age. The faint light of sunrise blossomed across a red and orange sky. There were no clouds and no noise, other than a few birds telling us they were up and ready for the day.

After a brief argument with myself about getting into a car with a stranger, the practical and safe me lost. I wanted to get home. I followed the man and found the ability to keep up fairly easily. I had vitality, and power, so strange after months on my back. Harley aimed the fob at a Rolls Royce in a doctor's spot in the staff parking lot.

"You're a doctor?" I asked by thinking, not speaking.

"Nope," he responded the same. "I'm a developer. Just found this fob on the counter back there and figured no one would be needing this any time soon. The car's been here all week, hasn't moved."

"Oh," I thought. I shrugged my shoulders and hopped in the passenger side. I've never been an accessory to any crime and found it a little exhilarating. I sunk into the soft leather of the luxury car. I had never ridden in a Rolls Royce, especially not a flying Pal-V Liberty Rolls Royce. It was something I could get used to. The car had to be close to half a million dollars-worth of steel magnesium alloy.

"Address?" He asked.

I gave him the information, which he punched into the Inertial nav system. The car lifted off the ground and accelerated out of the lot. There was no traffic on Crown Valley. The Rolls cruised through the yellow blinking traffic lights. As we passed the strip malls, I noticed the empty lots and broken windows. Some of the businesses had been boarded up. My sleepy little town of Laguna Niguel looked like a war zone. Fear rocked my gut. I felt like I'd traveled to a different country or a different time.

"My God," I said.

"I don't think God had much to do with this," Harley said. "They think it was the Russians."

I let Harley's words sink in. What had we done? The world shifted. Man playing God.

We approached Niguel Road and I grew more anxious. He put on the left blinker. I wondered why he bothered when he'd been ignoring all the traffic lights. Must be habit. The car coasted the rest of the way to our ranch style house in the hills overlooking the ocean.

"Nice digs," he said. "I live in the next development over."

"Thank you so much for taking me home," I said. I realized I needed to find out how to reach him. If so many people had died, we would need to know how to survive, and it looked like Harley had figured a few things out. Again, he seemed to know what I was thinking.

As he pulled up to the front of the house, he looked over at me and said, "I will come back later today. I can help with the next steps, like food and water, the important stuff."

"Thank you so much," I said, hardly able to express my gratitude for his help. "I'll see you later today." I was grateful he offered to come back. I felt as though I was swimming through the unknown.

As I got out of the car, my daughter barged through the front door of our house and hurled herself at me. Brittany hugged me so hard, I could barely breathe. I hugged her back, then took a close look. She was a whole half-foot taller than the last time I'd hugged her. Now Brittany stood a few inches taller than me. Her blonde hair was long, pulled back into a ponytail and she had on blue princess pajama bottoms with two sweaters over her pajama top. I waved good-by to Harley and the Rolls glided away from the curb.

"I'm so scared, Mom," she said. "I was afraid you were dead, like everyone else." She looked thin and frail.

"I'm so sorry, my little girl." I placed my hands on her cheeks and looked into her blue eyes, puffy, and red.

She started crying again. "I tried calling the police, but they never came."

I gave her another hug and we managed to get into the house. It was chilly. In Southern California, October can get cold, and this morning had to be in the fifties. Once inside, I stopped and listened. There was noise, like white noise, so many people talking all at once. But there was no one else in the house. Strange.

"What is that noise?" I asked.

"What noise?" Brittany looked confused. She pulled the rubber band out of her hair and cocked her head to one side. Her hair cascaded over one shoulder and fell, like silk, down to her waist. I shook my head and focused on my girl. Maybe this was another side-effect of the virus. When Harley and I talked telepathically, I only heard what he wanted to send to me.

What I heard now was muted random chatter. Brittany grabbed my hand and guided me to the kitchen.

"Where are you getting food?" I asked. I struggled to stop the noise in my head. The talking and chatter spun around in my mind. A wave of sadness gripped me, and I gave her another hug. I missed Larry, I wanted him to hug me. I wanted him to take care of this. He was always fixing problems, something he was good at.

"Once I finished almost everything in the cupboards and freezer in the garage, I raided the neighbors' houses." She pointed to the refrigerator. "We still have electricity, I guess because of the solar." Thank goodness we'd decided to go for the solar 2500 option with the new Graphene 10 battery to be conscious of the environment. We never expected it to pay off this way.

We both sat at the kitchen table next to the large picture window which looked out over an overgrown yard and a green pool.

She said, "I don't go to the houses with orange panels, like ours." She referred to the distinguishable twelve by twelve orange roof panels we'd installed when the new technology came out. No need for the grid. The energy was stored in a renewable battery, the size of a quarter. Brit wiped her eyes and gave a meek smile. "I can't tell if someone is home or not, but it seems as though more have survived in houses with the Orange solar panels."

"My poor girl," I said. "I am sorry you were alone."

"Well, I was not quite alone," she said and stared down at the table.

"What do you mean?" I asked.

"They are helping me," she said, but didn't look me in the eyes.

"What do you mean, they?" I asked.

"They're in the basement." She drummed her fingers on the table, impatient with her slow mother.

"Brit," I said quietly, not sure where to go with this. "We don't have a basement." Had she lost her mind? The seclusion and drama of the virus would hurt anyone's psyche.

"But Mom," she stood and grabbed my hand. "We do." My lack of understanding elicited an eye roll followed by an exasperated sigh.

She got up and pulled me to the back hallway. The spare bedroom door was shut. Brittany stopped and pushed the door open. The spare bedroom was gone. In its place was a set of stairs descending into a dark void.

"See," she said. I heard the noises very clearly now. They emanated from the new basement. The rumbling noise grew in my head, drawing my hands to my ears to stop the pain.

"Brit," I yelled over the din. "Who or what is down there?"

"They came while Dad was here," Brit said. "Mom, why are you yelling?"

"They are making so much noise," I shut the door. "Who are they and what are they?"

Brittany leaned against the wall. "They said you would come, but I didn't believe them. You were gone for so long." She sighed and waved her arms. "They said you, and others like you, with what you can do, will save us."

I narrowed my eyes at Brit as I tried to understand how my world had changed and how I could save us. I opened the door again and stared into the dark void and focused on the noise. As I listened, the talking and chatter became a tone, and the tone had meaning. It slowed, softened, and became one. That is when I knew what I had to do. My daughter, my neighbors, those that were left, the town, and the world, their future rested on my shoulders.

Demon

Lisa Richter

Every morning for months, Sally strolls the park adjacent to her apartment building, weaving among the tall trees, speaking to no one. A safe place, with all the open air.

From the shadow beneath a nearby leafy sycamore, a languid voice crawls: "Hello, Sally."

Her pulse jumps.

A bulldog with an amputated front leg hobbles into the sun. Josh follows.

The wavy gray hair, once cropped around his face, falls inches longer, and combed back, flips at the nap of his neck. Sandals, loose jeans, collared shirt. His standard attire, she remembers. How long has it been? A year? A midnight blue bandana pulls snug over his nose, mouth, and chin, bandito style. Oversized aviator shades hide his eyes, a deep coffee hue she knows.

His face covering is so complete, she wonders briefly if she could be mistaken, perhaps this isn't Josh at all. Some imposter, a thief, wearing Josh's hair and clothes. A madman with a bulldog who learned her name. Just that morning, the news reported a robbery at the local Starbucks. The officer called to the scene asked for a description. "Two guys in jeans wearing dark masks," the proprietor said, shaking his head. "Like everyone else."

An arid breeze rattles the overhead leaves and whips Sally's sundress against her thighs. Months in isolation have left her unable to begin a conversation. *Please go ahead and unmute yourself.* How many times had she heard that inane phrase these months online? *Can you hear me? Hello? Unmute yourself.*

Even if she could, what would she say?

Behind her, neon plastic-weave fencing surrounds the park's kiddie playground. The basketball hoops are gone, though the stark black poles remain. The undoing happened during one of Sally's walks, and like so much else lately, brought with it a discouraged sigh.

"Things have changed," Josh says.

"Yes," Sally says.

They are standing on opposite sides of a wide footpath. A small, elderly woman approaches. She wears a mask like Sally's: sleek, black, suffocating in the day's heat. A scraggly mutt at her side sniffs Josh's feet and the two saunter on. The bulldog observes, nonplussed.

"Is he...new?" Sally says. It would be like Josh to take in a crippled dog, solely to garner lively praise from others. *How good-hearted he is! How selfless!*

Cynical, she chides herself. Change, no matter how unlikely, is always possible. Life these past months is proof.

"Rocky," he says. He strokes the dog with the bottom of his foot.

He tells Sally his mother is trapped in a nursing facility in the Dakota hills. No visitors allowed, none. He planned to drive there and sneak in, he says. His mother, after all. Sally knows he says this to convince himself it is the right thing to do. To convince her he has a conscience. But it's a marathon haul to North Dakota, he adds. And now—he gives the dog another foot swipe—he has Rocky.

Teen boys, each carrying a box of pizza, race along the path. They are mask-less, like nearly everyone in the park under twenty. Sally unconsciously holds her breath to avoid any deadly exhales as they pass by.

A younger boy pulling up the rear, beefy and breathing heavily, pauses in front of Josh and extends a hand toward Rocky. The beast growls, an imposing force even with just three legs, and the kid runs on.

"How's Rosa?" Sally says, finally.

I'll never forget this, Josh told Sally, studying her body the morning he left Sally after five intense months to be with Rosa in LA, Rosa, who (a few years shy of Sally's forty) giggled like a pleased child, Josh said. Rosa, who was never sad, Rosa who *skipped.* That was before the airborne demon arrived. Before the hiding began.

"Back in Vancouver. She's a citizen there." Josh picks up a blackened tennis ball near the tree and lobs it a couple of meters into an expanse of grass. "We planned to get out together, but shit, they sent me back at the border."

And Rosa, good girl, skipped on.

Rocky hobbles to a metal post and lifts his leg. A remarkable act of balance. "Keep six feet distance", the sign implores. Twin stick-figures wear masks and stand on either end of a horizontal arrow.

Sally's chi healer, she discovered last month, is a rebel non-masker.

"Believe you are strong," he told her with a stunning display of shining teeth, "That is all you need."

His calm, exposed face unhinged her.

"But people are dying from this thing," she said.

"The weak are always dying, Sally," he said. "Do not fear."

But Sally does. She fears something immediate and visceral: her sanity beginning to wobble. In the blurred, run-on hours, she seeks out Beethoven for comfort. Slammed with numerous ailments, deafness being just one, he managed to keep going until age 56. "I am never alone when I am alone," Beethoven said. Unable to sleep, Sally sits at her piano with vodka on ice and begins again and again the tormented opening of the Pathétique. DA! da DA da DA dah... channeling, fortissimo, his un-aloneness.

"Have you lost your mind?" a neighbor more than once screamed and pounded on Sally's apartment door. "It's fucking after midnight."

Rocky crosses the footpath and sinks at Sally's feet with a satisfied grunt. He licks her toes. Maybe she should pass on Beethoven—I am alone when I am alone, she decides—and get a dog.

Harsh laughter wafts from the slope beyond the once-basketball courts. The pizza boys. Theirs is a wild freedom, Sally thinks as Josh takes a step closer, his six-foot frame approaching the danger zone. Above the park along wide branches, crows quietly assemble, anticipating the feast of leftovers.

Josh removes his shades. The dark, lazy eyes watch her, hold her. But something in them is not right. Sally senses a feverish heat. She tightens her breath.

"Sally...."

She surveys his lithe body, wonders if he still shaves evenings rather than mornings, whether gray stubble bristles against the inside of that cloth. She wants to ask why he's sought her out, what he expects from her now, after Rosa. But she knows. He takes another step. Then another. The subtle scent of tobacco, the mint soap. Sally tries to imagine his full face and is at a loss. She can't, no, her mind finds only his mouth, remembers only his lips, how their touch excited her skin, how they devoured her body. A heavy sweep of hair falls to his forehead. He leans in, reaches out. In the trees, crows flap about, impatient, as the boys' laughter soars.

Maximum Life Span

Dianne Russell

Onelia reads *The Merck Manual of Diagnosis and Therapy*, all the time now, as if her life depends on it. "Oldest continuously published medical textbook," it says on the cover. Onelia presumes they know what they're talking about, and she'll somehow stumble onto the cause for what's making her feel peculiar these days.

Settling into her living room chair, she plucks a clump of gray cat hair from the gap between the cushion and the armrest, sticks it in her sweater pocket, and opens the book to Section L. She's pleased that she's already halfway through the 2018 edition.

"Average life expectancy has increased a lot, but maximum life span has increased little if at all," states page five of Section L.

Onelia, who at 80 is past the point of average life expectancy of 78.54 years, tries to make sense of it. The length of anticipated life has increased, but the finish line is still where it always was? A puzzle to ponder.

But that was before the pandemic. Nothing is average now.

A year ago, no doubt she'd figure it out, like a formula in the algebra classes she taught for 30 years, but now she couldn't balance the two elements of that statement in her head. One does not equal the other.

Two of her widowed neighbors passed due to the virus, and they were only in their sixties. She's sure they expected to live well past that.

If only Jaco had lived a year longer—which was certainly possible since the maximum life span for an indoor cat is 17 or more—he'd have kept her company, just as he had for the 10 years since her husband died.

She remembers hearing that outdoor cats live an average of just two to five years. To be sure, their average life span hasn't increased. Trying to figure out the odds, the percentages of life expectancy for a feline that lives indoors compared to outdoors, Onelia divides 17 by 2, but the numbers ping around in her head like pinballs in an arcade game and, deciding it doesn't matter anyway, she gives up.

During the past week, as she entered the living room, she glimpsed Jaco curled up in the chair, as plain as day. Sometimes she even smelled the acrid odor of his litter box but discounted both the sightings and the odors as residual effects of being alone for two months.

Weeks ago, Onelia came to the conclusion that there was nothing to do now but read and already she's reread all the books stacked on the handmade shelf—which teeters off-kilter on one wall in her small apartment. Once the pandemic began, she canceled cable television, the one luxury she allowed herself after Jaco died. Although she collects a pension and social security, she convinced herself not to spend money on nonessentials. "Who knows where the country is headed," her husband always said.

Onelia kept her cell phone service so she can Facetime with her daughter and grandchildren two thousand miles away. Nevertheless, it flusters her seeing them on the screen.

After hearing on the radio that it's reassuring to tell youngsters they will come out the other side of this horrible virus situation, on their last Facetime call, Onelia told her grandsons what it was like to live through the polio pandemic.

"No one knew where the polio virus came from, so everything and everyone carried the possibility of a child spending the rest of his or her life in an iron lung. Every time we had a body ache, upset stomach, or headache, we suspected it was polio. They said maybe it spread through contaminated feces or gutter water, but no one was sure. So just like now, there were no outings or birthday parties or graduations. We were quarantined too."

From the looks on their faces, Onelia sensed her grandsons were bored with her story and cut it short. "You'll get through this polio epidemic just like we did," she said.

"Mom," her daughter said, though not in a condescending way, "this is a different epidemic, it's coronavirus."

Thinking of that conversation now, she should have told them it was better back then, at least she'd had her family to quarantine with—they played endless games of Canasta and watched "American Bandstand."

A knock on the door.

"Who is it?" Onelia says. But she knows it's the grocery delivery boy, who will not be there when she gathers up the food, so no need to bother with a mask. She hopes he didn't make another mistake like last time when there were six cans of cat food in the bag.

Onelia unloads the groceries, searching for the turmeric capsules she ordered after hearing on the radio that it helps with inflammation. She read a study led by a UCLA professor, stating that loneliness and social isolation can increase inflammation and decrease immune capacity.

No turmeric capsules. No choice but to call the corner market again.

"This is Onelia Cartwright. You forgot the bottle of turmeric in my delivery," she says.

"Sorry, we'll get it right over to you."

Onelia goes back to reading her Merck Manual, searching out the section on isolation.

"In 1972, French adventurer and scientist Michel Siffre famously shut himself in a cave in Texas for more than six months—what still clocks in as one of the longest self-isolation experiments in history. Meticulously documenting the effects on his mind over those 205 days, Siffre wrote that he could 'barely string thoughts' together after a couple months.

By the five-month mark, he was reportedly so desperate for company that he tried (unsuccessfully) to befriend a mouse.

"Research has shown that chronic social isolation increases the risk of mental health issues like depression, anxiety, and substance abuse, as well as chronic conditions like high blood pressure, heart disease, and diabetes. It also raises the risk of dementia in older adults."

Another knock.

"Finally. It's about time," says Onelia.

When she opens the door to retrieve the little bag left on the doormat, Jaco slips out, his body brushing her leg. As fast as she's able, Onelia chases after him, down the flight of stairs to the entrance door where he rushes out as the delivery boy exits.

"Get my cat," she yells in a voice as thin as her bones, but the boy is already gone.

Visible through a glass partition in the door, Jaco sits on the curb next to the light post, licking one front paw then the other before he saunters away.

Without even reaching into her pocket for her mask, Onelia decides, "What the hell, I'm already on borrowed time, 1.46 years to be exact," and pushes open the door to follow Jaco—his tail whipping with fear or joy—into the fresh air and welcoming space of the vacant sidewalk.

Letting Go
Catherine Singer

February 2, 2020

At the beginning of Sunday service, Nilla reached over and held my hand. It marked a change between us after twenty-five years of friendship. We both still carried the pain of losing our parents early and unraveling the madness of their alcoholism and mental illness, but we also shared a love of travel, adventure, the outdoors, and sushi.

While our minister delivered her message, Nilla squeezed my hand, looked into my eyes, and smiled with a tinge of sadness. Her eyes said, "I love you. I'm going to make the most of my shortened time." Chemotherapy had thinned her fine, Swedish, blond hair. Her cheeks had hollowed. After being confirmed cancer free three years prior, her breast cancer reappeared in her bones and liver.

I squeezed her hand in mine, reaching beyond my fear of intimacy and sadness of losing her. I smiled, thinking, *we only have the present moment.*

After the band wrapped up with the last song of the service, "Let There Be Peace on Earth," she moved her hand to my wrist. Her expression steadfast and happy. "I love you, my friend," she said.

"I love you too," I replied. Then, our friends engulfed her in hugs and hellos.

July 27, 2020

Nilla died four months later. She spent her last month searching for a miracle cure that took her to Arizona and then Texas, away from her many friends in California. The cancer had advanced to her lungs and stomach by the time her body gave out, just three days after a twenty-seven-hour train ride from Scottsdale to Houston.

Her sister Sylvia and significant other, Dilan, chose to honor her through a YouTube memorial. Dilan hired a company to produce the event. Six people at our Center for Spiritual Living presented live in the sanctuary. Dilan put together pre-recorded videos from friends. Sylvia assembled a slide show after sorting through 40,000 images she found on Nilla's phone and received from friends. Seventy-eight people attended online. At that time, gatherings for funerals were prohibited under the governor's COVID-19 mandate, but our minister, with great apprehension, allowed ten people in the center.

I hadn't planned to speak at her memorial until 3:00 that morning, awoken by an urgent need to say a few words about my cherished friend.

Letting Go

I sped into the parking lot and ran from my car with nine minutes to spare before our 10:00 a.m. start. Nilla's friend from her younger days of hang gliding and parachuting calmly greeted me in the shade by the sanctuary door. Patience and serenity filled her tan face. "Breathe," she implored, holding a spray bottle in one of her blue latex, gloved hands and a packet of disposable towels in the other. She had been assigned microphone cleaning duty.

A vision of sparseness hit me as I stepped into the nearly empty, high-ceilinged, one- hundred-seat room. Five friends, wearing surgical masks, sat scattered throughout the mauve colored space.

I knew two of the three men working the soundboard by the back wall. In the middle of the room, a silver-haired stranger tapped away at his laptop keyboard. A black video camera hung from a tripod over his left shoulder.

Dilan rushed up to me, appearing anxious. "Can you watch your cell phone for any glitches in the transmission?" he said. I wondered why he didn't trust our silver-haired stranger, later introduced to me as Marshall, to streamline the live and prerecorded parts of the event.

Sitting five rows back from the front, I immediately began fanning my face from the heat of the stage lights and bright July morning. Our petite Reverend Sunny carefully navigated the carpeted stage steps in her five-inch heels. The silk of her mottled, emerald green dress and shawl billowed behind her as she approached the microphone. Pushing a few strands of her blond hair behind an ear, she waited with the rest of us for Marshall to count down to the start.

"Ok. We're ready," he said. "Three. Two. One."

"Hello!" Reverend Sunny's voice boomed from the speaker as she smiled brightly. "And welcome to our Center for Spiritual Living to celebrate the life of our beloved Nilla Lindgren. First, Reverend Ari will light the Flames of Faith."

I looked down at my phone screen as Reverend Sunny named the essential beliefs of nine world religions, "Including the one that brought you here," while Reverend Ari lit the candles. White text messages from some of the seventy-five online attendees scrolled down the black screen. Hellos from Sweden, England, Iowa, California, Florida, New York, New Jersey, and more.

"Love you! Miss you, Nilla!"

"Miss you, Sister!"

I had to practically shake Marshall to tell him the online video transmission hadn't started. I saw, on his laptop screen, my deceased friend's mouth moving without sound. Her face was pale and gaunt in the bright Scottsdale sunshine where she, Dilan, and her sister spent three of her last four weeks. A heaviness filled my heart. *She made this video knowing she'd soon be dead,* I thought to myself. *She's so brave.*

"We need to stop," Marshall said, interrupting the candle lighting ceremony.

We waited a few minutes for another countdown. Then, Reverend Sunny repeated her introduction. Reverend Ari re-lit the candles. I watched Nilla's prerecorded message cut into the candle lighting ceremony, again.

After a Don Henley song played, Dilan spoke. He stepped onto the stage, raking his hand through his thick, black hair. "I've known Nilla over twenty years," he began. Soon, his voice cracked and tears streamed down his brown face. "She was my best friend. She made life a fun adventure." He choked back a sob. "She was always so positive." Then, he doubled over, silently crying for a moment. I held my breath, watching him, having never truly seen the depth of his love for her.

Looking down at my cell phone screen, I saw a text, "So good to see Dilan, if only a few seconds." Another, "Wish I could hear what he's saying." I gave up. The memorial would be a confusing mess. Nilla would have laughed.

A slide show began with an image of her bundled in a one-piece, black ski suit at the top of Mammoth Mountain by the former lip of Cornice. It was the most difficult entry into the mountain's black diamond run. In another picture, Nilla sat with Sylvia and her husband on a rickshaw that raced along a street. A former boyfriend of Nilla's stood on the back with a large smile. A slew of images of her and another ex-boyfriend scrolled by. I had no idea they dated for so long. Then came one of her and Dilan dressed up in black and white for a cabinetry awards dinner where she won Top Seller eight years in a row.

My turn to speak came sooner than expected. It irked me Dilan's daughter hadn't arrived. She only lived twenty minutes away.

I shared how our twenty-year friendship started when we met at my ex-boyfriend's fortieth birthday party. Nilla's sister worked with him and introduced them after he and I broke up. Nilla and I became fast friends through our shared love of the outdoors.

"Love, laughter, strength, beauty, courage, and commitment made up Nilla's essence. She would try to make the best of a difficult situation," I said to the camera. "She took chances with her art, be it painting on silk, with watercolors, or drawing. Her love was deep and strong. She accepted the people she loved, for better or worse.

"Once she came out to meet me for a Joshua Tree weekend with friends from my ski club. She immediately connected with people she hadn't met before and we had a blast. Lots of laughter, drinking wine, being exceptionally silly, watching the stars, and, in the day, hiking in the blazing heat.

"I realize now, that I'd known her at the end of a very vibrant and adventurous life. I would've loved to have gone on adventures with Nilla. Going out to sushi, walking, and hiking were our adventures.

"What still shines is her true spirit. It is a bright turquoise blue, a high frequency of love and light. It's a hummingbird that began to show itself outside my office window two days before she died and continues to care for the flowers in my garden. That is her true essence. Her friendship was a blessing," I concluded.

When I walked off the stage and sat down, Donna sprayed and wiped the mic. Finally, Dilan's daughter sprinted through the side door.

Dark black, grown out braids on one side of her head bounced as she raced up the stage steps. Three weeks of post-shave covered the other side. She slowed down, panting, and walked to the mic in her torn jeans, half-tucked black t-shirt, and jean jacket.

Her talk revealed a maternal side of Nilla I'd never known. How she brought this young woman's broken family back together, helped repair her relationship with her father, and never missed an important event in her life. I remembered Nilla and Dilan flying to Brazil for the wedding of Dilan's daughter and her girlfriend. Nilla was thrilled she could fit it in between her chemotherapy treatments.

Towards the end of the memorial, Marshall posted a video of Sylvia and her singing Happy Birthday in Swedish, a blessing she gave all her close friends on their special day. Despite her shortness of breath, Nilla sang for my significant other's birthday the previous April. In the video, the two sisters looked like a couple of girls playing a type of dress-up. Nilla's surgical mask, on top of her head, obscured her baldness. Sylvia wore hers over her chin.

After the video, Reverend Sunny returned to the stage and thanked our virtual audience for coming. Marshall said loudly, "That's it."

My joy of seeing Nilla again immediately vanished, replaced by a feeling of emptiness. Our fun times were over. The silence of her absence mixed with memories became our new present moment.

The morning of disjointed silences, tears, sanitation, confusion, while missing the warmth and support of our spiritual center's fellowship, made at least six of us yearn to extend our time together. I called a nearby restaurant and requested a secluded table. Instead of placing our group in the back, by a bridal shower, they opened their front patio by the parking lot for us. I pulled our three tables four feet apart, and we each sat with our "safe" partner.

A cool breeze blew through our spot in the shade, away from the hot blaze of the afternoon sun. When our drinks arrived, we took off our masks and toasted, "To Nilla. May she fly free in her next adventure."

Antimatter

Marrie Stone

These were nothing-to-lose times. Graham doesn't have to watch the news to know it. As he often tells his clients, "the wolf is at the door."

Though he spends the bulk of his days barricaded against the outside world, he still has to eat. Graham straps on an N95 over his grey beard and walks Portland's Pearl District from his riverfront high-rise through downtown and back across Waterfront Park. Smoke from the distant fires fills the skyline, making it uncomfortable to breathe.

He passes the bagel shop that burned in June, wondering when something will be done about it. Restaurant doors once locked, looped with ropes of chain and thick padlocks—one by one—have emptied and closed altogether. All the plate glass windows are still out in the Apple store, replaced by black plywood painted with angry graffiti: "BLM" and "Fuck the police" and "Lock Him Up." Nearly 200,000 dead Americans to date. *Seriously,* he thinks, *lock up that son-of-a-bitch.*

Crossing Pioneer Square, a reedy man with an addict's accent hops a cement blockade and follows Graham at a distance too close for comfort.

"We wearing masks now?" the junkie says. "Even outside?"

Graham walks faster and the man speeds up to keep pace, coughing on the back of Graham's shoulder.

"You drank the Kool-Aid, buddy. Stop acting like a fucking sheep."

Graham raises his tweed cap and tips it toward the man. "Will do," he says.

The man begins baaing and keeps it up until Graham rounds the bend. Everyday rage feels real.

He isn't afraid of confrontation—he's been a litigator for thirty-four years—but he learned long ago the art of choosing his battles. If he engaged with every lunatic on Portland's sidewalks, he'd find himself yelling all day.

Still, Graham can feel the rage rising in him, too. He feels the edges of his temper fray, the fibers of human decency starting to give way like reliable jeans too often worn. The only thing holding him together is Claire. Had they not met eleven months ago, he wonders at the man he'd be today—another middle-aged, rich, white guy with anger management issues. Though he hasn't been able to see her in months, the mere idea of her settles him down, gives him hope. Like a mental focal point, Claire's face a grounding force.

He huffs his way through the fall leaves of Waterfront Park, his beard itching beneath the mask, his mind worrying her like a wound. Graham wasn't a homewrecker. Claire had come to him seeking divorce advice. Recommended by a mutual acquaintance, Graham granted her the first hour free.

Spent. That was the word she'd used during their consultation. She felt spent after twenty-four years of marriage. Their only boy was out of the house, and she was young enough—early fifties (if fifty-three could be counted upon as early)—to write another chapter. "There's still time, isn't there, for something else?" she asked him.

Graham had done what he always did with new clients. He talked Claire through the unpleasantries of divorce, the occasional regret he'd seen in his clients' faces after the process was over and papers signed, the unexpected reversals of emotion. He wanted her to know, he said, "feelings could be temporary." It was best to take time and think this through.

"What about you?" she asked him. "What's the wife of a divorce lawyer like?"

Seldom in his career did Graham's face flush. Litigators trained themselves to give little away. But something about this woman made him want to give everything away.

"Haven't you heard?" he said. "The law is a jealous mistress."

"I haven't."

"Let's just say Lady Justice has ended a lot of marriages."

"So, you're divorced?" Claire leaned into his desk, the shadow of small cleavage beneath her white blouse, a suggestion of lace.

"Thankfully no. I never gave marriage a chance," he said. "Not to mention, this job will jade you."

"Well," she said. "Lucky you. Do you ever regret it?"

He'd pondered that question before—did he regret it? The truth was, not until lately when a kind of later life loneliness had set in. His friends joked about the benefits of bachelorhood, but they went home to wives and kids, busy with the daily obligations that added up to a lifetime of satisfaction and pride.

Graham was no stranger to sex, to divorcees, to the occasional woman committed to her freedom, but rarely did he engage in real relationships.

Claire slipped Graham her card as she left his office, her fingertips lingering on the inside of his hand, her warm skin sliding across his wrist before she let go. Coldwell Banker, a real estate agent. He should have known she was in sales.

"If you're ever in the market," she said. "That's my personal cell."

Graham found himself having to take his own advice, examine what it was about Claire that had him up all night, replaying their conversation, the look she'd tossed across his desk with eyes that leveled him, the way her serene face reminded him of home—as if her heart already held his memories, his thoughts, his secrets. How had he felt some shared history between them after only an hour in her company?

He referred her case to a colleague and asked her to lunch, still not intending for anything to happen, but needing to uncover what it was about Claire that had made him feel she was the singular woman he'd held out for his whole fifty-eight years.

That was last October, almost a year ago, five months before a microscopic virus upended the world. Before peaceful protestors took to his neighborhood and federal agents began abducting private citizens into unmarked vans. Before a series of wildfires claimed half his state.

Graham looks across the river at the east side of the city, still obscured by smoke. They hadn't had a real talk since the end of August, almost a month ago now, when he arranged a mid-morning call during Michael's daily run.

"He's still here," she'd told Graham. "It's too hot out. I'll call you later."

But Graham had already waited two weeks for this call. He wasn't going to give up without a small fight.

"Tell me," he said. "Do you still feel spent?" He rushed the question before she had a chance to hang up.

Her voice had been a whisper, locked inside her guest room bath with the sink running. "What?" She sounded annoyed.

"When we first met. In my office. You said your marriage made you feel spent. Drained or depleted. I just wondered."

"I don't know what I feel now. Numb, I guess. I guess I feel numb."

"You want to meet? I'll bet I can fix that." He lowered his voice to a timbre of seduction, trying to conceal his rising desperation.

"It's too hard to get away. Where would I be going? Nobody leaves."

"You need to tell him."

"Graham." His name in her mouth stopped him. "It's not the right time."

"That's how people stay stuck, love."

"Okay." She flushed the toilet. Additional cover, he imagined. "I'll call you."

"I love you."

"You too."

"Always."

The phone clicked off before Graham had a chance to ask what "you too" meant. It meant, he knew, she was slipping away.

Graham carries his bag of takeout from the still-surviving delicatessen. He nods at the doorman, waits for an empty elevator, and rides it up the fifteen floors to his condominium that, on clear days, looks across Portland's skyline towards the Willamette River. For all its mahogany wood and modern art, it'll never be enough to insulate him from the outside.

The twilight gloom hangs heavy outside his windows, the penthouse enveloped in the smoky haze from six separate fires that still have the city surrounded on two sides. His only view now is his reflection. He stares at it a moment before deciding he doesn't look well. He's drinking too much, eating too little, sleeping not at all.

He slumps in front of the theater-sized screen until the news repeats itself, Rachel Maddow announcing the same alarming stories, with the same expressions of rage, she'd reported three hours before. A lowball of bourbon sweats on the table beside him. He burps a potent mixture of pastrami and booze.

He texts: *You awake?*

Message delivered, he stares at the screen. Nothing. It's been three days without any reply, but still, he tosses texts at regular intervals like hopeful bottles into the cyberspheric ocean. He scrolls back up the string of their one-sided communication to see if he's said something wrong. Mostly it's pathetic displays of overwrought emotion ("I miss you" and "I love us" and "We'll be together on the other side"). Every endearment has been met with silence. Maybe Michael finally knows.

At 10:38, he tries for something less emotional. *Did you see they're talking about bringing back the feds? The goddamn National Guard. If this town isn't turning into some sort of police state.*

Nothing. Not even the floating bubbles of acknowledgment that his words are being received.

He's well into his fourth finger of whiskey by midnight when he clicks open Claire's contact information and opts out of the text, goes recklessly for the phone. If the world has become a dumpster fire, maybe it's Graham's turn to bring some gas.

Straight to voicemail, but he decides—contrary to his promises to her—to press ahead. His voice is low with the smoke of the distant fires and a thick coating of booze.

"I was thinking about our first date down at Nostrana's," he says into the automated abyss. "You said it wasn't a date . . . because married women don't date. Remember that?"

Graham closes his eyes, leans back into the brown leather headrest. He can still see Claire outside the restaurant, standing on the wet sidewalk in her thigh-high boots and camel cardigan. Her tiny frame looks more like a teenager than a middle-aged woman, her chestnut hair still thick with curls. She's laughing as she leans into his hand on the small of her back, allowing him to guide her to his car.

"You called it a get-together." He feels her breath in his beard, the brush of her lips like wings on his neck in the elevator. "You were right. We definitely got together. I've never felt that together. Not in fifty-eight years has someone gotten to me like this." He's fairly certain his words are slurring into each other, but he pushes on.

"The thing is, love, the thing this whole bloody mess has made me realize, is that life is short. And unknowable. And, frankly, frightening. I don't want to waste any more time. It took me half a century to realize what I want, but now I know." He pauses. Takes another draw on his drink. Feels himself inside her—the perfection of their fit, the way they anticipate each other's pleasure, each one coming to rescue the other before their needs fully arise. Graham knows, through shared instincts or some secret language between them, where to move his tongue and how to guide her fingers, simply by reading the sounds of Claire's breath.

He's aroused, losing himself in memories, before realizing he's alone. "Call me," he says. "I love you."

It's 1:43 a.m. and nothing. No response. No text. One more try and he'll drive there. That's what he'll do. He'll help Claire do the hard thing. They'll tell Michael together, and though it won't be pleasant, it will be done.

He talks himself into his Mercedes at 4:30, taking his time to carefully enter her address into his GPS and easing the sedan through the empty streets. He hasn't driven for several months and needs to stop for gas. He's drunk, but he's not dangerous. Still sober enough to maneuver the nozzle into the tank by the third try. He knows to keep to the speed limit, to obey every law and sign regardless of the emptiness of the roads. He also knows—if it comes to it—a fair number of lawyers and judges in town. On Interstate 5, he flips the A/C to high, powers down his windows, and blasts some Miles Davis.

Claire lives outside the city, in a southwestern suburb of middle-class homes. He parks a few doors down at the end of a cul-de-sac and kills the lights. Even in the dark, twin porch lamps illuminate the silhouette of her two-story tract home. Rarely has he allowed himself to imagine her house. He navigates the driveway on whiskey legs, aiming for the weather-worn wood of the front porch, the faded welcome mat inviting visitors to "Wipe Their Paws," the trio of ceramic rabbits clustered in one corner under the awning, and a kitschy set of wind chimes rusted with age.

This isn't how he imagined she lived—domesticated, with a penchant for tacky middle-class clutter. This whole scene is what he's worked his life to avoid. The Claire he knows favors silk blouses and French perfume, leather handbags that accent her expensive heels. His mind had pictured her inside a Stickley-restored craftsman or maybe something modern, industrial—glass and steel to match her sharp intellect and internal strength. Instead, twin American flags, the size of postcards, flank her mailbox. He never figured her for a flag-waver. But never mind. There are mysteries left to learn, and he'll enjoy discovering them.

He settles himself on her porch swing to wait, sinking into the unpleasant purgatory bourbon always brings, the unsettling point on the inebriation spectrum when the booze drains from his brain and into his liver, the numb buzz giving way to what he knows will become a heavy hangover.

As the red sun rises into the smoke-filled sky, Graham dismisses his discomfort and lets his imagination wander. She'll be awake soon. Then they can begin.

• • •

THESE WERE EVERYTHING-TO-LOSE TIMES. Claire doesn't need to scroll her newsfeed to know it. She hasn't sold a house since March. Michael's company announced lay offs in July. Seventeen years with the same architectural firm and no severance package. Their health insurance gone—poof!—just like that. Robbie has been exiled from Stanford's campus after only one year, forced to learn Latin, economics, and calculus online from his childhood bedroom. While Claire continues transferring hefty sums out of a 529 plan they worked two decades to fund. There's looting, rioting, and goddamn Antifa with their militant agenda destroying her hometown. Wildfires are licking up the western United States. Then there's Graham. Claire can barely breathe.

Still, if she's honest with herself, certain things have gotten better since the pandemic began. Her marriage, for one. For the first time since Robbie was born, she finally has time with Michael. Neither one of them sleeps much anymore, so they stay up all night watching stupid movies together and pass out until hours she hasn't seen on her alarm clock since college. They've got nowhere to be except together, and there's been comfort in their shared struggles.

She stands at the kitchen sink, slicing yesterday's small harvest of strawberries into a spinach salad. It's still too smoky to eat outside, so she sets up the dining room with candles and cloth napkins. The table had been her home office until last spring, stacked with piles of papers and files, her printer consuming the whole far end. Michael ate at the office or picked up takeout on his drive home. Claire fished pre-prepared foods from the fridge, standing over the kitchen sink and eating out of plastic containers to avoid the hassle of dishes. Robbie hadn't eaten at home since he got his driver's license three years ago. Now, every night is a family ritual—silverware and candles and her mother's china. She makes things nice where she can and hopes it compensates for the rotation of simple leftovers.

"Looks delicious," Michael says. He pulls back her curls to kiss her neck, his face newly shaven, his breath a burst of mint. This, too, is new. Until the global pause, Michael and Claire could go for weeks without physical acts of affection and think little of it. Over the decades, their sex life evolved from frequent and frenzied, to steady and comforting, to occasional and efficient.

"That's marriage," Amy told her one night last year while trying—not for the first time—to pour another round of Chardonnay from a long-empty bottle. "At least you're still having sex." Wine became a small seawall of protection against the rising panic of Claire's newly emptied nest. Amy had been beside Claire through every high and low tide—her maid-of-honor, her oldest high school friend, the trusted lockbox for decades of shared confidences.

"I'm not complaining," Claire had said. "It's just an observation."

"No one observes something they're happy about."

Claire wondered on the long walk home, whether that was true. She decided to test Amy's theory, putting renewed effort into her marriage. She traded her Adidas for alligator heels, Burt's Bees for *Lancôme* lipstick, Target panties for Victoria's

Secret. In the end, the sex was just as efficient, and the exercise felt like . . . effort.

"In the words of Billy Joel," Michael told her one night, dropping his briefs at the foot of their bed, but not bothering with his t-shirt and socks, "Don't go changing, babe."

But Claire liked the changes. She bought more lingerie, this time for herself. She indulged in a small bottle of Chanel and one pair of Prada's on deep discount at Nordstrom Rack. Her conversation with Amy had planted a seed. Now that her only son was gone, maybe efficient was no longer enough.

Her phone vibrates in the back pocket of her jeans. Then again. Then three times more.

"Someone must want you as much as I do," Michael says, squeezing her ass before disappearing into the pantry to retrieve a bottle of merlot. For a man nearly fifty-five, Michael has held his physique. He's still within their wedding weight, owing to a daily five-mile run. Genetics gifted him with thick hair, still more pepper than salt. The lines around his eyes add a sense of wisdom and maturity. Whatever their problems, she's never lost her attraction to him.

"Can you pull the chicken out of the oven?" Claire says on her way up the stairs. "I'll be down in a minute."

Her phone vibrates again on the landing. Though she still hasn't checked it, there's no doubt who's texting. She hasn't been able to bring herself to answer him, nor can she bring herself to block him. Even Amy doesn't know about Graham.

She crawls into the master closet, closes the door, and slumps to the floor. All the texts have come from the same unknown number, well known to Claire.

There is this: *I know you, love. Better than you know yourself. I know what you're worth. What you deserve. Who you can be. If you let me, I'll show you. Just say yes.*

Then this: *I know you're not a woman who needs rescuing. But every rescue operation needs a support team, right? I'm here.*

And this: *I've been thinking, when all this craziness blows over, we should spend a few months at my place in Gordes. It's not much—an old stone cottage down near Marseille—but it's enough. We can regroup. Plan our life. Eat. Drink. Make merry.*

Finally, this: *Whatever you're thinking. Whatever you're going through. I get it. But don't give up on us. That's all I ask.*

She loves how he texts. Full sentences with perfect punctuation. For a lawyer, he can sound a little like a poet—sensitive and insightful. He makes her feel seen. Makes her feel both smart and sexual at once, appreciated for her brains and her beauty. He brings out her best self and makes her believe this is the woman she's always been.

The first time she glided up those fifteen floors into Graham's glass condominium, Claire did feel like some rescued princess. All that exquisite art. All those leather-bound books.

"You've read all these?" Claire paused at the floor-to-ceiling bookcases that lined the largest room of the penthouse, more shelves visible in the dining room behind the wall. She would come to discover his bedroom walls bulging with nonfiction—biographies and business manuals, science and history, and art. Thick treatises on philosophy lined a large shelf in Graham's master bath, a stash of paperback thrillers in the kitchen, and old law school hornbooks stacked in two precarious piles in the hallway closet. She couldn't decide if his home looked like a modern art museum or the central library.

"More or less," he said.

"I'm guessing more."

"What can I say?" He came up from behind and handed her a drink in a glass that probably cost more than her car. "I have plenty of curiosities, a lot of time, and few obligations."

Claire pulled a book at random from a middle shelf. *Antimatter* by Frank Close. "What got you curious about this?"

"Who isn't curious about quantum physics?"

"Not this guy." Claire said, with a playful smile. "Hasn't he decided it doesn't matter?"

"Funny," he said. "Turns out it's a useful book for divorce lawyers. Matter and its natural opposite—antimatter. But what I love is the poetic science behind it. The elegant metaphor. The idea that there's this bizarre mirror world where every particle has an identical opposite. Left and right, positive and negative, up and down. Whenever the two meet, they annihilate each other in a massive explosion on a scale the brain can't fathom. What's not to love about that?"

Who talked like this, Claire had wondered. Everything about Graham felt this way—charged with intellectual energy and curiosity, like the best college professor she'd ever known combined with the most sensitive artist. She couldn't think of a witty retort, so settled on: "A little like you and me?"

"You think we're opposites? I hope not."

"I think what we have could destroy everything." It sounded stupid, false even as she said it, overdramatized and a little cheesy. But she was trying to keep up her end of the banter.

"Maybe what we have would just create something new."

"That sounds like a single man's point of view."

"It's the only point of view I've got."

Claire hears Robbie's guitar through the wall. He's improved in the last six months, doing little else in his room but practice. It's a healthy obsession that stirs her pride and makes her marvel at the man her son has become.

While Robbie locks himself away in his room, Michael spends his empty afternoons at the rifle range. He'd been an amateur marksman when he was young, duck hunting trips with his uncle as a kid and, later, wild game with his fraternity buddies. But once the unrest started in their city's streets—when protestors busted up the courthouse and looted their friend's jewelry store—Michael bought a semi-automatic pistol and a .38 special.

"We need these for what?" Claire asked him.

"Boy Scout motto, babe. Always be prepared."

Michael prepares three times a week now. "Threat Dynamics LLC" appears more often on Claire's credit card bill than her weekly groceries.

"You're spending money we don't have," Claire told him last month as he got in his truck.

"Consider it an investment," he said. "Insurance."

"I don't like it."

"You'll like it when you need it." He slammed the door, ending the conversation.

She doesn't even like being in her closet anymore, with Michael's old shelf of tennis shoes now replaced by a small safe stuffed with heavy boxes of ammunition. But since the riots began—their small suburban neighborhood suffering a spate of break-ins and vandalism—Claire suspects Michael might be right.

Graham is nothing like Michael. She can't imagine Graham owning a gun, let alone using one. It makes her both respect him while wondering if he isn't a little naïve.

Her chest aches as she deletes Graham's texts. Too risky to keep them, but also painful to let them go. She feels stuck in every way—unwilling to cut Graham loose and unable to leave Michael. Their shared history means something, decades of memories impossible to toss away.

But maybe Graham is right. Maybe the west is burning and a virus is raging for some bigger reason. Maybe forcing people to pause and consider the world—their place in it, their responsibility—is long overdue. Maybe something better and new isn't such a bad thing.

She'll wait before responding—give life another day to reveal some answer. "Inaction is a form of action" her mother used to say. But the price of any action feels insurmountably high. The sound of Graham's voice would be her undoing.

"Mom," Robbie calls from his room. "Come listen to this."

Claire powers off her cell phone to silence the insurgency of messages and climbs out of the closet. She slips the phone into her nightstand, where she keeps a small locked box of mementos from her months with Graham: a plastic hotel keycard from their one weekend in Cannon Beach, paper menus and restaurant matchbooks, a quartz rock they found on a walk, a used cocktail napkin with a rough sketch Graham drew of Claire's profile, and a sapphire necklace he told her to keep until she made up her mind.

"Be right there."

Claire also spends more time with Robbie now than ever before. When he was a baby, she bristled at his bottomless needs demanding her scarce energy. But she loves the young man he's become—smart and creative and full of masculine initiative. She sits long hours listening to him play the guitar, takes an interest in his gaming the way she never had time to do before.

"That's really coming along," she tells him. "You should do a recording. Share it around."

"It's not there yet," Robbie says. "But who knows what can happen with another few months at home."

"Dinner's ready," she says, lifting herself off Robbie's bed. He needs new furniture, at least a man-sized mattress if he's going to live back home. And where's the money for that?

She rejoins Michael downstairs, moving the salad bowl from the kitchen counter to the dining table while he carves the small chicken into thin slices that he spreads across a platter in an effort to make it appear enough.

"What was that all about?" he asks.

"What?"

"All those texts," Michael says. "A house lead?"

"Maybe." Claire feels herself stiffen, her mind running through the list of pre-canned excuses she used to rely upon. Those days feel ages ago. "We'll see if it pans out."

"Just don't tell me you found a boyfriend," Michael smiles. "A guy hates being kicked when he's down."

She forces a laugh, turning into the refrigerator to avoid his gaze as she searches for salad dressing. "Unless I meet someone in our living room, I doubt you have much to worry about."

"You never know," he says, kissing the back of her neck.

"I'm pretty sure I do."

"You're a naughty one," Michael whispers. "And you know it drives me crazy."

After dinner, Michael proposes a Will Ferrell marathon, and Robbie retreats to his room. She settles her head into the crook of Michael's solid arm. They make it through *Downhill, Land of the Lost,* and most of *Zoolander* before turning back to *Good Day Oregon,* as the sun starts to rise. The Fox morning news team assures them the firefighters are slowly gaining ground against the worst of the blaze. The Lionshead Fire is ten percent contained, and there's a promise of rain in the next few days.

"Hang on, Portlanders," the newscaster tells them. "Things are about to turn."

"We could use some good news," Claire says, but Michael has dozed off. She lets herself bathe in the blue light of the news, feeling the renewed rise of hysteria under her skin. Some stories make her want to hunker in their basement and wait out the worst of it. Others make her want to take to the streets and fight. Sometimes she thinks, *fuck it. Let's burn the damn country down to the ground and start over.* The pinball of emotions exhausts her, the uncertainty about where things are heading and how they'll get there. Who will survive and who will succumb.

"We should go upstairs," she says to Michael, rubbing his arm awake. "Try to get some rest."

He mumbles and stirs beside her, but eventually stretches himself up and off the sofa. He takes her hands and lifts Claire to her feet, slipping his arms around her waist and pulling her into him, cocooning her into his chest. She wonders, standing inside this circle and drawing in his strength, if this is enough to save them.

They make their way to the front of the house, through the kitchen and past the living room windows, pausing for Michael to check the deadbolt on the front door.

She loves this time of day, the quiet peacefulness of it, the hopeful possibilities that dawn always brings. Smoky sunlight is starting to stream in through the sidelights, and it catches on Michael's face, giving him a morning glow.

He pauses, then turns back towards her. His shoulders tense, and his arms rise up in a posture of confusion or self-defense.

"Claire," he whispers, "There's someone on the porch."

She's beside him at the glass. She sees Graham's tweed cap resting against the hard arm of their swing, his beard a soft grey against his black sweater. His arms are crossed at the chest, his eyes closed behind glasses he didn't bother to remove.

"Get the Glock," Michael says, pushing her back away from the window.

His words arrive in a rush. She tries reconstructing them, calculating Michael's overreaction to such a benign threat, wondering what he suspects and maybe has known all along. If her mind had time to form a complete thought, it might have been this: What if this is the miraculous moment that ends it all?

But the only word she can muster is, "What?"

Rats, Bats, Chickens, and a Blue-Eyed Cat

Laurie Sullivan

Caroline feels the pressure of a mounting body count and the promise to her father before he passed of COVID-25, so she pushes on despite the guilt of working too many hours.

The thirty-six-year-old Cornell University PhD graduate sits at the table in the lunch area of the Hong Kong Institute of Infectious Disease. It's two o'clock on Thursday morning. Tacked to the wall, a digital clock that flickers April 10, 2025 like a neon sign about to burn out.

In rice paper, she wraps small pieces of sweet and sour pork remaining from her dinner, carries it into the lab with the animals and stuffs the bits through the rats' metal-mesh cage.

"We all need a bit of comfort these days" she tells them. Chickens, bats, and other animals look at her as if to ask, "Where's mine?"

One rat grabs the mesh with its retractable claws and rattles the cage to ask for more, but Caroline dismisses the request.

"Next time," she says, wagging a finger. "No more."

With a pull on the lab door behind her, she rounds the corner and plops in the chair. A tap on the glass panel from her desk says, "I'm here if you need me." Rats, chickens, and bats stop eating and fussing to listen and stare. The tom cat jumps into Caroline's lap. She softly strokes his head, as he falls asleep.

Caroline's attention gets pulled from the animals by a flash of light on the computer screen. A sequence of numbers and letters run across the bottom of the browser too fast for her to read. An article from *The Wall Street Journal* appears, reports more than 200,000 new cases worldwide yesterday. It reminds her why she took on the project six months ago, as her father succumbed to the disease during early stages of Parkinson's.

The last few days of her father's life they spoke about many things. They talked about his love for cats and books, and how the world had changed during the past six years.

"I couldn't save you, Dad, but I might be able to save others," Caroline says, blinking back tears.

She made her father a promise, to approach finding the source of the virus with the strength and the stamina of a dragon slayer. The type described in the books he read to her as a child. Born in Lecompton, Kansas, with a population of 625, Caroline and her father explored the world through books.

"Crap," she says. The computer screen goes dark. She turns off the machine, reaches behind the desk to pull the plug, counts to sixty, and hits the top of the monitor twice with a palm for good luck. Then plugs in the machine and turns it on.

The blank screen intensifies the pressure she feels as days tick by without a possible cure or proven vaccine. She feels it, too, from the lack of research funding by the Hong Kong government based on the number of people dying each day, and the promise to her father made before he died. The pressure and anxiety sometimes become unbearable, but she sighs with relief as the hard drive reboots and the monitor shows signs of life.

With bird-like arms, pale from a lack of sunlight, Caroline pushes her chair from the desk. The rollers stick, then glide effortlessly with a slight squeal on the cold grey-tile floor. At four o'clock in the morning, she gets up and stumbles before filling her cup from the hot-water spout in the kitchenette. Glancing in the mirror above the sink, her hazel eyes widen. She looks for jaundice in the whites of her eyes and skin tone, both early signs of the virus.

Her cold hands wrap around the porcelain cup. The black tea bag floats for a bit before it succumbs to the liquid and sinks to the bottom. A splash of coconut milk from a small mason jar in the refrigerator tops off the hot liquid. She takes a sip, but her favorite black tea with a hint of honey and blueberry tastes different. Almost no taste at all.

This should get me to sunrise, she thinks, but her lids feel heavy and warm—much warmer than her hands and her nose, which chill when she's sick.

Caroline tries to shake the drowsiness from her head. Her wish for swift vengeance on the assholes who allowed so many to get sick or die from the virus increases her anxiety. She wants to break the window and scream, "Fuck you, fuck you," into the darkness, but doesn't. She stares out the window, studies the empty street and imagines another life, another story behind every pane of glass and front door.

Behind Hong Kong's façade residents live under China's oppression, where many have become wary of the future. They struggle with inherent online bias guiding their culture and a belief system that undercuts democracy. The seed sown in March 2019, at the start of the Hong Kong protests.

Caroline inhales. The air fills her lungs. A tickle in her throat forces a cough.

Out the window and down the street, she looks for her favorite restaurant, Jan Jan Kushikatsu. It's where she and Leonora, Rupert's wife, enjoyed dinner the last time they went out with friends in February. Since then, Hong Kong announced the virus as a pandemic, closed businesses, and locked-down and restricted residents from travel.

Jan Jan Kushikatsu also is where Caroline and her colleague, Lenora, from Minneapolis met the American engineer from Silicon Valley. He clued them into a somewhat related project during a chat and a shot of sake at the bar. He said machines were being taught to not only learn from, but capitalize on human emotions. In a semi-drunken state, he spoke about a little-known theory.

For years scientists thought that one day an unknown virus, with no known treatment or cure, would originate in a string of computer code, jumping from machine to human. It would spread fast based on the amount of time people spent staring at screens.

Leonora and Rupert stepped into the institute several months ago to assist in locating the origin of COVID-25.

As part of the U.S. team who discovered the origin of COVID-19, they would return in the morning, when the clock ticked seven, to resume the search. Their findings helped Russia develop the first vaccine in 2020, but Caroline vowed to aid in finding the origin and the cure to this pandemic.

The rooms at the Institute remain stark and empty except for Caroline and the animals. The rats, the chickens, the bats all in separate cages. Rats run in rhythmic circles, chickens cluck in hysteria, and battered bats flap their clipped wings. Caroline spins her chair, looking at the four walls in the biggest cage of all—her office—as the animals follow her movement through the glass partition.

Caroline's scrawny lab cat, a black and white tom with unusual blue eyes, spends mornings winding his body and tail through the legs of Caroline's chair. He stops in a strange way to shake with each purr. The shakes keep the garbage-bin rescue skinny.

For a few seconds, Mr. Cat meets Caroline's eyes, as if to ask for permission to jump up for a nap. Caroline pats her thigh and the cat leaps.

Despite Mr. Cat's warmth, Caroline shivers and wipes her brow with the back of her boney hand. Her breath becomes shallow, labored. She crosses her arms on the desk in front of her computer. Her head becomes heavy. She closes her eyes for relief.

The air conditioning blows, but the sweat collects and breeds behind her knees, in the crease of her forearms, and crick of her neck.

She dozes off. A voice wakes her. "Did you find it?"

Caroline quits breathing. Doesn't suck another breath until she manages to get out, "Who said that?"

"I did," the voice says.

"Who's 'I'?" Caroline looks through the glass partition in the adjacent room with the animals.

"Down here," the voice says. "I'm in the other room behind the glass partition in the cage."

"Do you all talk?"

"No, just me," the rat says. "You do know you're infected with the virus, right?"

"Yes, but I can't give up." Caroline reaches for a tissue to wipe dripping sweat from the back of her neck.

"It's not every day you can have a conversation with a rodent," the rat says, pausing. He looks up at her from the other side of the glass. Wiggles his nose and whiskers, and scratches behind one ear like a dog with dry skin.

"So, did you find it?" the rat says. "It's right under your nose. In fact, if it was a snake it would've bit ya. Probably gobbled me up, too."

"A rat with a sense of humor."

Caroline opens a browser. She stares into the screen allowing the built-in scanner to read her retina, which will log her into the Institute's research search engine. Before she can log-in, another flash, another strobe.

This time she doesn't blink. Her eyes open like camera lenses, taking in the flash and image. She manages to get a glimpse of the computer code running across the bottom of the screen—Waiting for api2.branch ... https://adclick.g.doubledouble.net/click/fire. Another flash. She feels a tingle in her eyes.

"This is it," she says. "The code explains how the virus infects humans."

Caroline dials Rupert's mobile phone but gets voicemail and starts to leave a message.

"I found it," she says, as giddy as a teenage girl with her first car. "It's based on ambient biometrics, which identifies the characteristics of a human and its surroundings before transmitting the virus from the computer screen's retina scanner."

She gets up and walks to the kitchenette and looks into the mirror above the sink.

"I can see it through changes in my pupils, tiny changes of color in my face, tiny bobs of the head and flairs of the nostrils," Caroline tells Rupert, tilting her head from side to side. "The retina scanner seems to estimate the oxygen in the blood. The code is verifying the transfer of the virus. It's in the code at the bottom of the computer browser."

From the code, Caroline can tell that the virus gets injected into the computer browser to infect the person looking at the screen.

"The device accepts the code, reads it, and turns the sequence of letters and numbers into the virus," she says. "It sends the code through the retina reader into the victim's eyes. The code then seems to turn into a virus that invades living cells and uses its host's metabolic processes to produce a new generation of viral particles."

The stamp at the end of the code reads "Nightshade," she tells Rupert before pushing the button on her iPhone to end the call.

"Bingo," the rat says.

"It's as quick as a click," the chicken says with a cluck, scratching its hock on the grated floor of the metal cage.

Caroline turns from the computer screen to look into the rat's red eyes. "I thought you were the only one who could talk," she says.

"I'm a rat," he says. "You should expect duplicity."

"You're also a know-it-all, Mr. Rat, so I expect you to, well, know it all," Caroline says, tapping the heel of her right foot on the tile floor, making a restless clicking sound and stretching her neck toward the computer as if to peck the screen with her nose like a chicken. "A little modesty would also help."

Caroline grabs her tea in hopes it will snap her out of the drowsiness, but the cup slips from her hand. It hits the tile floor and explodes into tiny pieces.

"Watch it," the shaking cat says, looking up at Caroline.

"I'm sorry, Mr. Cat, come here," Caroline says, trying to calm him.

She reaches for Mr. Cat, but he looks up at Caroline in disgust, turns, and walks the other way, swishing his tail.

Caroline covers her mouth. Another cough comes. This one with yellow phlegm. She shakes. Her throat tickles. She coughs again. It leaves a spatter of blood in her palms. Both hands move to her head. She coats her long brown strands in bloody clumps of mucus while squeezing her head to try and stop it from pounding. Her breathing becomes labored. A tingling sensation rushes her body. She can feel sores form on her face, worse than any acne she experienced as a child.

"Do you think she'll come back in her next life as a rodent, a bird or a feline?" the rat asks the chicken and the cat as he eats the last bit of nibble in his bowl.

Caroline struggles to reach her phone on the desk, as the animals watch. Weak and labored, she rests her head on the desk in front of the computer screen.

At seven, as the sun takes its place in the sky to welcome another day, Lenora and Rupert turn the deadbolt of the front door to the lab. She hears the tumblers in the lock move. She hears them walk through the hallway and into their shared office space next to hers.

Caroline hears every word and movement in the lab as the animals scurry. The sounds echo. The hard drive whines, as the computer clicks on. Rupert checks his phone for messages and tells Lenora he has one missed call from Caroline.

"My God, the flash from this old computer hurts my eyes," Lenora tells Rupert, as Caroline feels a tap on her hand.

"It's time to go," a man's voice says.

Caroline looks up at her father's stern face. She has come to appreciate his guidance more in death than in life. Isn't that the way it goes?

"Wait, hold on." Caroline looks around for Mr. Cat, her companion, to say good-bye, but he's nowhere to be found.

She looks into her father's bright blue eyes, and then at the picture on the desk of herself and the blue-eyed cat.

With a kiss on the tips of her index and middle finger, she taps the picture of Mr. Cat.

"I knew there was something familiar about you," she says.

Safe

Judy Wagner

The death rate exploded in early '95 and my neighbors, afraid of the mysterious virus, locked themselves in their homes. Most businesses in our quaint artists' village closed without notice. Fear shrouded my secluded coastal town like a silent gray fog.

When the ambulances stopped coming, a movie producer wearing a black hat with *Smitty* embroidered in white, went door-to-door volunteering his old faded red pick-up to transport the sick. One morning, across the street, a young couple carried an elderly woman from their home on a stretcher crafted from wooden broom handles and an old quilt. Once driven away in the bed of Smitty's truck, the afflicted never returned. More than half the houses north of Laguna Canyon now sat empty. The rest lost multiple family members. I was spared.

We expected to lose the elderly, but children disappeared just as quickly. Some in our enclave lost two, three, and—in one case—five children. Not everyone born after '72 succumbed to the outbreak, but most did. One afternoon, between gruesome descriptions of genocide in Eastern

Europe, a local anchor reported most people left alive had the smallpox scar on their left shoulder. I rubbed my arm. My '70s kindergarten class had been one of the last to be vaccinated. We would be some of the youngest survivors. I had just turned twenty-five.

In May, after Smitty and his guys blocked the only three roads into the village, they took guard to keep us safe. A few days later while on the deck drinking coffee, my neighbor with the high blond ponytail strode from house to house taping a notice to every mailbox announcing a meeting in Heisler Park.

I had watched the neighbor-parade from my rooftop perch each morning since leaving college in '89. A string of joggers, dog walkers, and groups of chatty women, strolled past each day on their way to the beach or village shops. Hunkered on my patio three floors up, I sat alone, in Grandpa's old teak chair, and envied the beautiful people and their beautiful world.

Ponytail Girl usually wore running shorts with an oversized sweatshirt and carried a white paper cup from the new trendy coffee house on Coast Highway. I recognized her as one of the it-girls from campus, thick long blond hair and bouncy step, her face the perfect amount of dewy no matter the temperature. Some days I thought I could smell Giorgio as she passed, but it could have been in my head. The swarms of girls wearing Greek letters on campus had all smelled like Giorgio.

The night of the meeting in the park, I wore my best jeans and a white long sleeve mock turtle that had hung in my closet, tags still attached, for longer than I could remember. I tamed my long brown hair with a thick padded headband like the one I'd seen President Clinton's wife wear. The new guise suited me. I looked plain but well-groomed and my neck was covered.

I sucked menthol Chapstick from my lower lip as I crossed Coast Highway, only fairly confident my black cotton mask concealed the thick rippled scars on my right cheek. I approached the bluff-top park and marveled at the powerful surf below. I recognized many of my neighbors milling about the grass, though I'd never met most of them.

About a hundred of us made it to the meeting that afternoon, most of us in our mid-twenties to late sixties. I hadn't been in a group that large since college, and even then, I'd avoided crowds. I enrolled in as many night classes as I could. They weren't as crowded, and I preferred to slink across campus in the shadows.

I stood on the grass in the back near an overflowing cement trash can stamped to look like it was crafted from pebbles. An old hippie lady, in a flowing tie-dyed caftan, collected discarded bottles and paper from the ground around the cement receptacle and dropped it in a used plastic grocery bag. The crowd spread out across the grass as if surrendering space to the invisible pathogen. I shifted my weight from one foot to the other and fidgeted with my mask, pulling on each side to ensure it covered me ear to ear.

The setting reminded me of the farm auction Grandpa and I visited during one of our trips to Nebraska. Smitty balanced atop an old wooden milk crate, pointed to neighbors in the crowd, and spoke quickly like an auctioneer. He didn't waste an ounce of energy. He sported long gray curls, distinctively California, and a surfer vibe with an authoritative slant. His look probably worked well in Hollywood. I'd noticed him around town for years. It was impossible to not notice him, an original, his look all his own. Not conforming to surfer or producer, he was himself and I envied him.

I'd worried for days about this meeting, what to wear, what to say, and all I intended to do was disappear into the crowd. The longer I waited for the meeting to begin, the faster my pulse raced. I tried to calm myself. I named objects in the park, something my childhood therapist taught me. *Palm tree. Black Doc Martens. Red bandana.* She said it would ground me in the moment, stop my mind from racing.

Ponytail Girl climbed atop the box after Smitty. "I'll lead agriculture," she said. She gestured with a green Lucite clipboard, undoubtedly color coded to match her task. She outlined a contingency plan in case food deliveries stopped. "If you've got gardening experience, meet me in the back," she said when she finished.

Grandpa had referred to his garden as top-notch. He'd rave over an especially perfect summer squash or compliment himself at the dinner table while devouring a salad made with his tender butter lettuce.

The crowd shifted into smaller groups. Ponytail Girl jogged toward me.

"I noticed your compost bin," she said.

I looked to the overflowing trash can and wondered if she was attempting a joke.

"I can see it in your backyard from my bedroom window." She laughed. "I'm not a stalker."

I raised my chin to look her in the eye for a few excruciating seconds, then returned to studying my Birkenstocks. I sucked in my cheeks and chewed the sides of my mouth, tried to seem nonchalant, as if the crowd and conversation weren't making me want to shed my skin.

"I'm glad you're going to help," she said. "I've never grown anything."

I hadn't offered to help, hadn't moved from my spot since I arrived. She chatted up volunteers who gathered in a loose group around me. Her mannerisms were too bold for someone who had just announced she'd lead a group on a topic she knew nothing about. It felt just like college where attractive girls and tall guys possessed unearned confidence.

"We need to be ready," she said, scribbling names and addresses behind her clipboard. "Our world is shrinking pretty quickly."

I'd never been a joiner because groups had meetings. I shuddered at the thought but gave my info in order to blend in with the others.

As my neighbors planned gardens and seed banks, I looked west over the ocean to Catalina in the distance. Growing up,

Grandpa and I had made many plein-air paintings in this nearby park, but I hadn't seen the island in more than a year.

When the group broke up, Ponytail focused her attention back on me. "Smitty and his guys have us locked down pretty good. Anyone who decides to stay can't come and go," she said.

"Come and go?" I said. In high school, Grandpa taught me how to hold a conversation so I wouldn't agonize about what to say. Repeat the last few words someone says, he told me, like a volley, get the ball back in their court. It always worked. Turns out, all people needed to talk about themselves was a prompt.

"You can leave, but they won't let you back in," she said.

I shrugged. I had nothing outside the house in Laguna.

"I think it'll be fine too," she said. "We'll be friends."

"Friends." I forced a smile under my mask. It would be nice to have a friend. I was certain Ponytail Girl and I would never be friends.

The next March, a few months after people started venturing outdoors again, when new infections leveled off, I agreed to teach my neighbor with the high pony my gardening tricks.

"You definitely have the best garden," she said.

"Best garden?" I said.

"I'm learning it's almost impossible to keep tomatoes alive this close to the beach."

My neighbor kneeled in the freshly tilled soil of what used to be my front lawn. We planted seedlings for about an hour before she asked about the small white dots speckled up and down my arms. My stomach tightened, and my breath stuck at the top of my throat. I could still see the looks of disgust when people first got a glimpse of my scabs and pustules, back when I was in school, in the '80s, long before the outbreak. I'd learned early on there was no way back from a bad first impression.

"I used to pick at my arms." I kept Ponytail Girl in my peripheral vision and steadied for her reaction while I continued to mix soil with compost.

She sat back on her Timberlands and surveyed her work. "When you were a kid?" she said, admiring the line of delicate green sprouts stretching about 10 feet.

"When I was a kid." I lied. I wasn't ready to share my eccentricities with my newly acquainted neighbor and her flawless ivory arms. That's what Grandma called my skin picking, my eccentricity, as if it made me an exotic party guest instead of weird and creepy. After Grandma died, my scabs turned to purple spots the size of a pencil eraser and, recently, they faded to colorless almost imperceptible scars on my newly tanned arms. I'd started wearing grandma's old short-sleeved T-shirts and dresses from the '80s. My thirsty white arms drank in the sun and ripened to a Coppertone brown I'd always envied on other Laguna Beach girls.

My neighbor touched my forearm with her leather gardening glove. I flinched. Soil from her glove mixed with my sweat and left a two-inch streak of mud on my arm.

"You're right," she said. "It's probably not safe to touch, even with gloves."

Her eyes crinkled around the edges. I could tell she was smiling under her emerald green cloth mask. We learned to read eyes in Laguna that first year.

"You play bingo?" she said.

"Bingo?" I said.

"Your shirt."

I looked at my chest. I wore a ladies black short-sleeved tee with over-sized shoulder pads. *Bingo Babe* was spelled out across the front in madras plaid appliqué letters. "It was my Grandma's," I said.

When news of the virus hit, old age hadn't yet taken Grandma. She had existed for two years in our second floor living room in a hospital bed paid for by Medicare. I hardly left the house after Grandpa died, afraid to leave Grandma alone. Then the virus put an end to hospice visits, and I started cooking with old canned goods that filled the kitchen cupboards.

One afternoon, before deaths in California hit ten million, a month or so before Smitty's roadblocks, Grandma slipped away while the TV reported a bombing in Oklahoma City. When the funeral home took her, I was left alone in the clutter. Endless mountains of Grandpa's treasures cascaded through every room in the house. Rolling hills of paper mixed with plastic shopping bags blended into piles of what my Grandpa referred to as family antiques. I recognized them as keepsakes from homes of dead relatives, hauled 1,500 miles from Nebraska to our home in North Laguna in the back of Grandpa's Lincoln.

I slid Radiohead into my boom box and went to work on the garage first. It took a few days to separate junk from anything still in mostly working order. Tools were relegated to Grandpa's built-in workbench, constructed more than thirty years ago when he regularly used his jigsaws and vice grips. I stacked endless cases of Costco paper goods, enormous bags of rice, and a case of stewed tomatoes, on wood-plank shelving in the narrow storage room off the garage. My enormous makeshift pantry would become infamous and indispensable to the neighborhood.

It took almost four weeks to get the house livable, even though I'd lived in it since Mom went away in '72.

I kept more than I would have, had the death toll not been skyrocketing. "You never know," I said, when I couldn't throw out a questionable item. It was a phrase that made me cringe every time Grandpa said it. Almost daily he'd bound through the door with an old rusty item he'd no doubt found at someone's curb, someone who knew the difference between trash and treasure.

Ponytail Girl sprinkled powdered eggshells into the remaining small holes she'd dug to plant the seedlings. "I'm not sure about these eggshells."

"Eggshells?" I said.

"Tell me what they're for again."

"Prevents blossom-end rot."

"My world keeps getting smaller." She laughed. Her ponytail swung as she shook her head. "Last year corporate compliance, this year, end rot."

"Blossom-end." I corrected her. "Rot at the end where the blossom is."

Her eyebrows raised and she cocked her head to one side.

Grandpa had taught me how tomatoes need consistency and a continuous stream of calcium during the early growth stage to avoid this type of rot. Without the right care, the tomato skin breaks down and turns leathery brown as the fruit starts to ripen. "It's to be avoided," I said, convinced I'd made an unforgivable conversational error. My instincts told me to run.

"How'd you learn all this anyway?" she said.

"Grandpa taught me. He grew up in Nebraska on a farm."

"And he lived here?" She pointed toward the house with Grandpa's metal garden spade with the dry gray wooden handle.

I packed soil around the final plants, intent to choose my words more carefully. "More like I lived with him and Grandma."

"Your parents too?"

"I don't have a Dad. Mom left when I was six."

"Do you remember her?"

"No." Another lie. I needed to put a stop to Ponytail's questions. "That's about it." I stood up and brushed soil from my bare knees.

"Tomorrow? Same time? My house?" she said.

"Your house."

I had moved in with Grandma and Grandpa in '71, after Mom had saved my life at least three times. Grandma reminded me of the fact anytime the subject of Mom came up.

The first time Mom saved me I was a toddler in the backseat of her used Impala wagon. I remember the color, turquoise, very popular in the early sixties. I don't recall if the wagon had seatbelts, but my suspicion is that it had old fashioned lap belts, and Mom hadn't buckled me in.

"You somehow got out of your seatbelt and got that backdoor open," Grandma would say. "She caught you by your shirttail. Going 35-miles-per-hour. Held onto that little shirt until she could pull over."

"I think I wanted out," I told Grandma once, having vague flashes of asphalt and curiosity, but not fear. Mom was always the hero in Grandma's stories.

I have a better recollection of the second time Mom saved me. A few months after my third birthday, according to Grandma, I slipped into a duck pond during a picnic in the park. I knew to hold my breath and opened my eyes like I did in the pool with the high school girls next door. I was excited to see what hidden world lurked beneath the pond's surface. The water was thick and brown like chocolate milk. It frothed and bubbled around me when Mom jumped in.

"Your mom's new outfit was ruined, you know." Grandma always mentioned Mom's new clothes and how the slimy pond muck ruined her Pappagallo sandals. Grandma lingered on Mom's bravery, marveled at how adept Mom was at saving me.

I, too, lingered on the near-death experiences, each one traumatic enough to imprint a lasting memory on a child not yet three years old. While Grandma painted images of a capeless superhero, I had visions of a picnic table covered in bottles, and an Impala filled with thick gray cigarette smoke.

Around five years after Smitty and his crew had blocked the roads, I finally told my friend with the ponytail about Mom.

"Did anyone think it was odd?" my friend asked, "Needing to be saved so often?"

"No one but me," I said.

She hesitated, then laughed from her gut in loud bursts. "No one but you." She fell to her elbows between her raised rose beds. "You're hilarious."

I let out a sneaky laugh, like a kid who knows she's been caught doing something naughty, but knows she'll get away with it. I raked gravel around a tiny bush that displayed a single thornless Sterling Silver rose. "Did you know this rose is the parent of all other lavender roses? It's the original. Difficult to get started but over time, once established in good soil, it's hearty."

"You know I knew nothing about roses before you came along." She clipped a pale yellow rose low on the bush, leaving a foot-long stem. "What was the third time?" she said.

"Third time?" I said, stalling. *Straw hat. Brown mulch, Denim cut-offs.* I listed what I saw around me while gathering my courage. I flinched, recalling orange flames, searing pain, and Mom's screams after she wrestled me to the grass. "In '71 we lived in the Canyon with some of Mom's friends. I was about to start kindergarten. It was a party, a cookout with Mom and her friends. I was excited for hot dogs. Well, veggie dogs, but they were still a huge treat, and Mom would let me cook my own. Someone tossed a Styrofoam cup full of lighter fluid onto the grill. It exploded."

My friend stopped pruning and looked at me, "Your mom pulled you out of the way? Saved you from being burned alive?"

"Something like that," I turned to my right, not wanting her to look too closely at that side of my face. "I haven't told that story in fifteen years."

"What happened to your mom?"

"She wasn't burned."

"I mean, where'd she go?"

"Away," I said. In Grandpa's house we never talked about where Mom went. Every few years Grandma got an unsigned letter postmarked from Thailand, or India, or some other location just as exotic, but we never discussed it.

"It's probably a good thing. If she'd stayed, you might not have made it to the third grade."

My new friend confirmed something no one in my family dared say aloud. I decided to continue before I lost my nerve. "Mom and her boyfriend fled the country before the Hippie Mafia was rounded up in '72."

"What?" she said, high pitched, staccato, like a Chihuahua.

I studied her closely, weighed her reaction, unsure if it was interest or horror I heard in her voice. "You know, LSD, Orange Sunshine, Timothy Leary."

"Your mother was mixed up with Timothy Leary and psychedelics? How have you not told me this before?"

"I've never told anyone before." Again, I needed to gauge her reaction, afraid I'd revealed something weird.

"You get more interesting by the day."

Smitty's truck crawled up the hill, slowing for a chat each time he saw an occupied front yard. He had become our operations manager. Daily, he ferried our local barter goods to the roadblocks. Lobsters, roses, and Pablo Honey, our branded honey from hives up on Spur Ridge, were the most sought-after items. He returned with whatever was available for trade, the day's government rations, and if we were lucky, a few day-old newspapers.

I was surprised at the high demand for our roses and honey, but after the outbreak, currency shifted.

"Missed you girls at sunset last night," Smitty yelled from the cab when the truck reached my friend's yard. He now sported a gray pointy beard and resembled King Neptune.

"It's nice to be missed," I said.

"Got some news at the roadblocks today." He waved a folded newspaper. "The smallpox variation seems to be working in LA. Ninety-eight percent they say."

This wasn't the first time we'd heard about a remedy for the mutating virus. In the four years since TV had stopped, we'd heard about dozens, usually by word of mouth. Baseless rumors that came and went as often as our ocean breeze.

"It's in the *Times*," Smitty said.

I sucked my bottom lip beneath my mask. An article in the *Times* suggested this treatment might be legit.

My friend grabbed Smitty's paper and scanned the front page.

"What does it say?" I asked.

"Works as a vaccine, gives immunity they think," Smitty said.

"They think," I said. In my head I ran immunity scenarios noting which ones would be more likely to take away my mask. "Broad immunity?"

"We'll see," he said. "Also got a message delivered with the paper. They'd like to try it here. Since we're isolated."

"Sounds risky." I rubbed my mask, tracing my finger along the pronounced ridges of my scars.

Smitty shook his head. "I already sent a message back. Told them 'hell yes.'"

"Says here immunity shouldn't diminish over time," my friend said. She searched for a new page to continue the story, folded the paper in half, and went back to reading.

"It just might cut the mustard," Smitty said, his commanding baritone more powerful than the truck's rough idle. "See you girls tonight for the solstice." He accelerated up the hill. Thick brown exhaust sputtered from the back of the truck.

"What are you going to wear?" my friend asked.

Our village gathered on the beach for a bonfire each summer and winter solstice. "Wear?" I said. What to wear was a pre-pandemic problem I thought had been solved for good. Smitty's vaccine news was already changing things.

"Get dressed up with me." she said. "My sorority used to have an annual Barefoot on the Beach formal. It's tons of fun"

She was already different, contemplating pre-virus priorities. "Fun," I said.

Grandpa's tools were scattered between the rose beds; his ancient rust covered hoe with the long thick wooden handle lay at my feet. My nose tingled. "Gotta run," I said, and left the tools as I dashed out of the yard.

Halfway up the hill I broke into a jog. Full guttural sobs hit me at the top of my street. My mask muffled my cries and sopped up the tears. The wails started as soon as my heavy red door shut behind me. If the article in the *Times* was right, masks might not be required. Beauty, money, and power would return as the ultimate currency.

After twenty minutes of naming items around the house, I'd calmed myself enough to think about the party. Before the outbreak, I had only one nice dress, a black long sleeve shirtdress I'd worn to Grandpa's funeral. Definitely not formal.

I modeled most of my closet in front of the full-length mirror on the back of Grandma's bedroom door. I even tried on one of Grandma's long muumuus printed with large red and yellow hibiscus. I looked like a clown draped in a circus tent.

It was almost dinner time. My nervous stomach wasn't going to allow me to eat before the party.

I checked the small guest room closet, sliding coat after coat out of the way before spotting the dress. Black velvet peeked out from below an old green wool jacket trimmed in fur. I recognized the dress from the picture of Mom on the old oak sewing machine cabinet next to the front door. A school dance, I think Grandma told me when I asked, but maybe I hadn't asked.

I held the fitted off-the-shoulder bodice to my chest and pulled velvet to each side of my waist. The full skirt swung with enough material to cover a petticoat. I'd trimmed down during the outbreak, my waist now well-defined between my small bust and wide hips. I stepped into the dress and pulled the zipper until it stopped between my shoulder blades. The black velvet dipped lower on my back than I'd expected. The bodice had a little extra room, but nothing a few staples couldn't fix. I strutted a few times in front of Grandma's mirror, like a model working the catwalk, then pulled up my hair and held it in a bun on top of my head. My reflection caught me off guard. I looked like Mom.

Gold watch. Flowered bedspread. Wooden jewelry box. I fought to keep the knot in my stomach from rising to my throat. My arms tingled. I jutted my lower jaw forward and held it firm. "You're nothing like her," I said to the mirror. "Nothing."

At 7:30 I made my way down the hill and across PCH. With each step I forced myself to keep from turning around and sprinting home. I'd pinned my hair in a tight twist at the nape of my neck, the scars on my right ear and neck visible. When I reached the path leading down to the beach, I waited on the bluff. Most of our North Laguna crew had already arrived. A bonfire blazed in a wide pit dug into the sand and circled with rocks. A boombox, hooked up to a generator belonging to one of Smitty's guys, blasted Gloria Gaynor. My friend with the ponytail danced with a large group near the fire.

"I will survive." They yelled the words to our adopted '70s anthem.

I stood on the bluff a few minutes until the sky turned pink, the dancers turned to silhouettes in front of the fire.

I wasn't positive I was safe. Maybe I would never be sure. My shoes dangling from my index finger. I made my way down the dusty path.

About the Contributors

Dina Andre quit a corporate career to focus on recent adventures. As a certified Grief Recovery Specialist, she helps people heal from loss. As a writer, she is working on her novel (found in the closet), bringing the characters to life. She's a member of Writers Block Party, a group of amazing humans and talented writers, mentored by Barbara DeMarco-Barrett. She writes short stories, poetry, and lists. And she loves llamas.

Cindy Trane Christeson is a freelance writer and speaker. She wrote a weekly column in *The Daily Pilot* called "The Moral of the Story" for 12 years, and a weekly Faith column in *The Newport Beach Independent* for 11 years. Her 10 years in Barbara's Literary Posse have greatly improved her ability to share help and hope to those in grief. Cindy's grief journey began when her daughter Amy died 13 years ago.

Angela Cybulski is writing a historical novel about the Bloomsbury Group during the early days of World War I. She has written for the *Dappled Things* blog, *Deep Down Things*, and is the author of the blogs *Persephone Writes* and *one tiny violet*. Angela most recently served as the managing editor for Wiseblood Books. She was awarded the inaugural Creative Arts

About the Contributors

Fellowship at the Hank Center for Catholic Intellectual Heritage at Loyola University.

Amelia Dellos is a storyteller based in Chicago. Her novel, *Delilah Recovered*, was selected out of more than 200,000 entries on the international platform Wattpad to win a 2017 Watty. As a produced screenwriter and director, her films have appeared on PBS and Amazon Prime, receiving the Sundance International Writer's Lab Finalist, Chicago International Film Festival Pitch Winner, and the Women's International Film Festival Finalist. Amelia lives just outside of the city limits with her husband, daughter, and two little dogs.

Barbara DeMarco-Barrett wrote the *Los Angeles Times* bestseller *Pen on Fire: A Busy Woman's Guide to Igniting the Writer Within*. Her stories and essays are in *Orange County Noir, USA Noir: Best of the Akashic Noir Series, Shotgun Honey, Crossing Borders,* and the *Los Angeles Times*. Since 1998, she has hosted Writers on Writing on KUCI-FM. She received the Distinguished Instructor's Award at UC-Irvine Extension.

Nancy Carpenter has been a contract writer for the mortgage, financial, insurance, and tech industries for 20 years. Which is to say she writes pretty boring stuff. The creative part comes in the form of novels. She is working on her fifth, as well as an occasional short story. This is her first stab at collaboration.

Phil Doran has been a Hollywood insider for more than 35 years, working as a writer-producer on such sit-coms as *The Wonder Years, The Bob Newhart Show, Sanford and Son, All in the Family, Who's The Boss?* and *The Facts of Life*. He's also the author of *The Reluctant Tuscan*, published by Penguin Books. He has written two stage plays: *A Couple of Guys at the Movies*, for The Tamarind Theater in Hollywood, and *Baby Boomer Blues*, performed at the PAC Theater in Laguna Woods.

Anne Dunham is a member of the Literary Posse and is working on her first novel. She took a detour that resulted in the story, "Legacy." In this short story, she wanted to explore broken relationships set against the backdrop of a global pandemic and how its deadly consequences affect those on the periphery.

Jennifer Irani is an artist, writer, and works as an elementary school special aid. The hope of her students, and today's youth movement to mitigate climate change, inspired her story. Her concerns about the environment, justice, and the need for compassion influence her writing. She always looks for the silver lining in the darkest moments. She is a member of Barbara's Literary Posse and has published her essays in local and national publications.

About the Contributors

Stephanie King is a member of Barbara DeMarco-Barrett's Literary Posse. Originally from upstate New York, she has been trying to adapt to Newport Beach, California, for nearly twenty years. *Community Spread* is her first short story.

Jan Mannino retired as a nurse anesthesiologist after a long and interesting career administering anesthesia for surgery and obstetrics. She remains active in the profession, where she lectures, consults and has written two books on anesthesia legal and business topics. She is also a law school graduate. As a retirement project, Jan has turned to writing fiction and is currently working on a book about medical malpractice.

Rosalia Rodriguez Mattern is an unapologetic book addict and a newbie writer, joining the Literary Posse three years ago. Rosalia is grateful for the opportunity to participate in this collection. "Womb" is her first short story. Her poem, "Treasures of a Simple Day," was included in *The Laguna Beach Anthology of Poetry/Short Fiction*. She's this year's third place winner in the John Gardiner Poetry Contest. Her essays have been published in *Orange Coast Magazine*.

Marla J. Noel spent 25-plus years in corporate life running several small businesses. The most recent business before her current consulting practice was a cemetery/mortuary, which she ran for 15 years. This helped to provide fodder for her current novel. Marla also dabbles in short stories, which range from creepy to YA. Marla has been a member of Barbara DeMarco Barrett's writing class and enjoys the break from her consulting practice, OC Growth Advisors, an executive coaching business to expand her reach into creativity.

Lisa Richter's poetry, essays, and short fiction have appeared in literary journals and anthologies, both in print and online. In 2014 she was selected as a finalist in *Glimmer Train*'s national fiction contest. She holds degrees in mathematics and creative writing and is a poetry alumna of the Community of Writers at Squaw Valley.

Dianne Russell is one of the original members of Writers Block Party. Although she's currently working on her second novel, *In the Midst of Things Broken*—which may or may not involve poisoning someone—she occasionally writes short stories and loves all things dark and off-kilter. For the past three years, she's served as associate editor/writer for *Stu News*, an online Laguna Beach newspaper.

Catherine Singer has spent a lifetime exploring the world around her through photography and travel. For six years, she wrote articles about AIDS/HIV issues and treatment for the *Laguna Beach* and *Long Beach Blade* magazine. Catherine is currently working on as photo essay of her experience with breast cancer. She's thrilled to be part of Barbara DeMarco-Barrett's Literary Posse.

About the Contributors

Marrie Stone is a former corporate attorney. Her fiction and essays have appeared or been accepted for publication in *Reed Magazine*, the *Writer's Journal*, *River Oak Review*, *Into the Void*, *Coffin Bell*, *The Rambler*, *The Write Launch*, and also in *Orange Coast Magazine* and various online blogs. She co-hosts the weekly KUCI radio show *Writers on Writing*, where she has interviewed more than 500 writers, poets, and literary agents.

Laurie Sullivan taps nonfiction and fiction techniques to write articles, poetry, lyrics, short stories, and novels. She has spent more than 20 years as a journalist for a variety of publications, covering trends and advanced technologies in high-tech electronics and online advertising, such as artificial intelligence and retina eye-tracking systems. With a Master of Fine Arts in Creative Writing from Chapman University, Sullivan helps her fictional characters travel through the unknown in search of answers.

Judy Wagner's first short story, *The Chipmunk Family*, debuted on her mother's fridge when she was six years old. Because she likes to eat and have a roof over her head, Judy worked in telecommunication and software sales for 25 years. She lives in Corona del Mar, California, and spends her time writing, managing her farms, and cleaning up after her calico, Tippy, and her five-pound Pomeranian, Sadie.

Made in the USA
Middletown, DE
12 November 2020